Looking Through Lace Curtains

Gregory Sayer lives and works in France. He was born in Hampshire and grew up in Petersfield before leaving for Nottingham University where he graduated in French Studies in 1976. He embarked on a career as a Language Teacher in Paris before retiring in 2016 to write.

First Published in Great Britain in 2021
by Lamplight Glow Publications

ISBN: 978-2-9576637-0-5 (Paperback)
ISBN: 978-2-9576637-1-2 (ebook)

Text design by Ellipsis, Glasgow
Back cover: Painting by William Gunning King, "Petersfield Square". Courtesy of the Royal Pavilion & Museums, Brighton & Hove."

Cover artwork by Damien Sayer, Berlin, 2021.

To Bénédicte, Damien and Jonathan.

Looking Through Lace Curtains

Gregory Sayer

LAMPLIGHT GLOW PUBLICATIONS

Contents

Family Trees viii–x

Prologue 1

Part 1
Journeymen and Rovers 7

Part 2
The Blood of Eden 53

Part 3
The Haven of Hope – That which *once* was Mine 89

Part 4
The Fourth Age of Man 191

Part 5
Pack up your Troubles 259

Epilogue 285

The Kimble Family

(Characters in grey feature in the book)

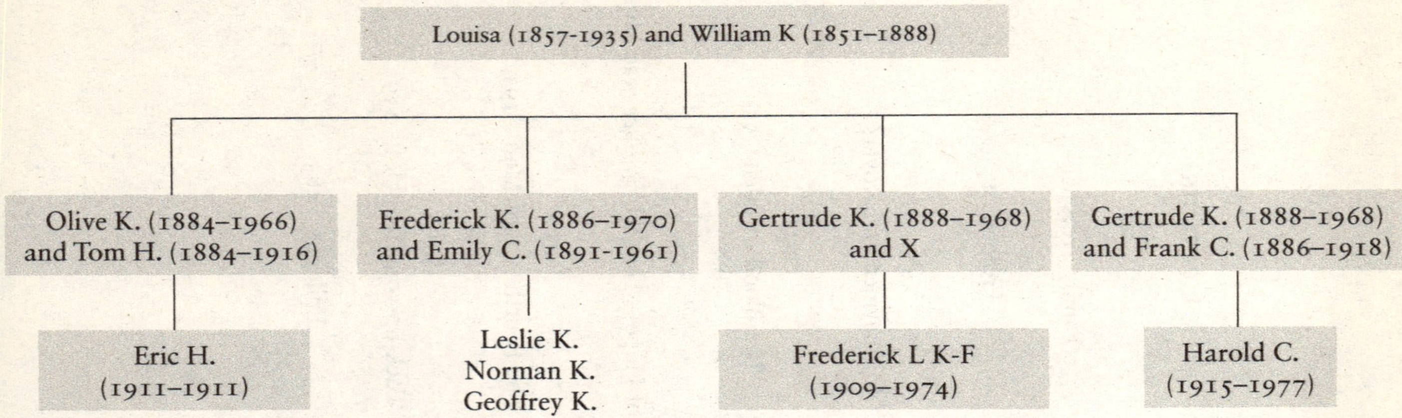

The Harding Family

(Characters in grey feature in the book)

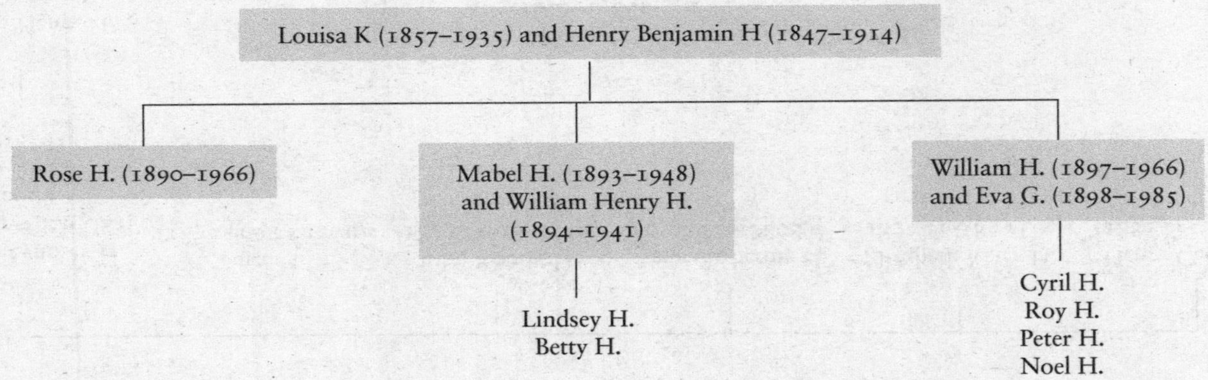

The Halden Family

(Characters in grey feature in the book)

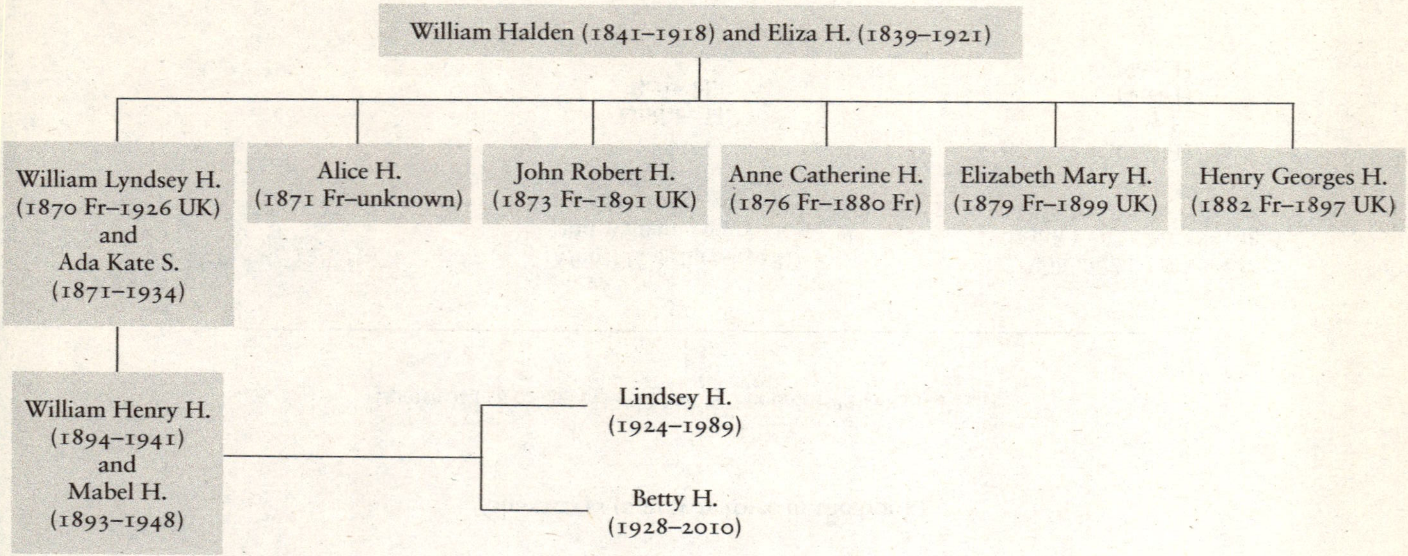

Note from the author.

This book is more fiction than reality but the writing of it is driven by my desire to explain, wrongly or rightly, a family mystery. The dividing line between fiction and reality is often blurred for two main reasons: absence of information and poetic licence.

Nevertheless, telling this story is vital.

The events are largely accurate. Such characters existed, their relations and their friends, too. They resembled millions of others whose ordeals were real and dreadful, going way beyond the bounds of fiction, which served as cement for me, sealing the gaps in this story.

The account traces the life of the ill-starred Maydurham family, the Kimble-Hardings, and their down-to-earth aspirations for happiness. It also follows the peregrinations and settling of the Halden family in Maydurham, later to be linked through marriage to the Harding side of the family.

Different members of these families emerged from the West Country, and moved east, some even travelled to live in France, but their focal point was Maydurham. Ultimately their destinies would be linked to Flanders, Germany, France and Australia.

These were my ancestors.

When they were much older and I was much younger, Gertrude, Olive and Rose lived in a little row of houses where their view of the outside world was somehow hemmed in by their lace curtains. If you, too, had sat with them in the quiet of their little front rooms, you would have understood both the shrouding of their windows and the stories they were loath to tell.

I regularly took the shopping to them and sat with them. I was just a schoolboy and they were my great aunts. We spoke of the present and I only heard the silence of the long gone past.

* * *

The research for this book has been painstaking, but it has put me in touch with new family and friends. Their remarkable willingness to help me piece together this book, our mutual care for family stories, as well as our love and respect for a generation not so long gone and whose fate contrasts so considerably with ours, underline the significance of the journey I undertook in writing this book.

The story has merely been sketched here, because neither a dictionary nor prose holds the words that depict the horrors some of them were destined to endure.

Perhaps music or art may have been more effective.

La connaissance du passé ressemblerait plutôt à l'acte par lequel à l'homme au moment d'un danger soudain se présentera un souvenir qui le sauve.

—Walter Benjamin, *Sur le concept d'histoire*, 1940, Ecrits français.

'Awareness of the past would resemble the act in which, in a moment of sudden danger, man would be presented with a memory that saves him.'

—Author's translation

Prologue

The flowers left thick at nightfall in the wood
This Eastertide call into mind the men,
Now far from home, who, with their sweethearts, should
Have gathered them and will do never again.

—'In Memoriam (Easter 1915)'
Edward Thomas

I stood at the top of the forgotten lane.

It separated from the main road, which wound down the hill into the town.

The lane wasn't so much a fork in the road as it was an abrupt change of direction.

It ran down steeply and I followed, engulfed in the tunnel of luxuriant bushes and tall overshadowing trees bordering the fields and backs of gardens. As if to avoid them, it turned left at a farm and descended in a long straight line beneath the trees towards a brook that had somehow submerged itself under a narrow carriageway, becoming a pond in a garden on the other side of the road. Half a mile later the same brook became a rush of a cascade before gurgling in happiness as it rode across an open plain.

Few ventured down this lane except local villagers on walks and hesitant runners. Many of these people kept to the lane, avoiding the occasionally muddy pathways that took you back up along the descending brook and into the hillside. Those walks demanded patience and effort.

Especially the walk alongside the brook, with its gradual but steady incline that took the breath out of the elderly and excited children with its steep banks. Cutting in and out of trees, its path skirted the top of fields and finally reached a commemorative stone that still sits at the crown of the hill.

Standing beside it, I surveyed the manor houses, farm-yards, and the rolling downs in the distance. I could see the town's rooftops and spire, the aging but now gentrified terraced houses that cut orderly lines into the more obscure rooftop arrangements.

This view and the natural silence of the wooded hanger had probably remained the same since the Roman settlement. Nature waits on no one, and then man encroaches. The town in the distance is called Maydurham because etymology has it that 'durham' sets the words 'town' and 'hill' together and 'May' is said to have been the remainder of 'mead', possibly relating to the age-old local brewing practices.

* * *

This all-encompassing view contrasted greatly with what little might be seen from the windows of the terraced houses.

They give onto the back of the old storehouse as well as a path, which runs down to a parallel road below. Inside, their front rooms are private and small, harbouring armchairs, a fireplace, lace curtains and shadows, only opened for guests and special occasions. The passageway goes past the front room to the kitchen that opens onto a small backyard, and then a limited patch of grass before you reach the back gate opening on to the back alleyway, running parallel to the railway line. Two up, two down. The same for all.

Right in the middle of this collection of terraced houses is an arched passageway leading to the back alleyway: practical for small wedding or funeral parties who do not have to traipse through the interior of the small house to its rear.

Standing in the backyard, you can hear the clickety-click of the train beyond the bank as it pulls out of the station and gathers speed, usually on time. A glance at the clock on the kitchen wall will confirm it.

* * *

If you descend into the town, find the flagstones of the churchyard and listen, only the wind in the trees welcomes you. Gradually, the sounds of the town and passing pedestrians fill the air. Here man has worked his architectural masterpiece into the geology of mother nature, benefiting from her slopes, streams, tree-lined hills, and marshy flatlands to create this dwelling place.

Centuries ago the Saxons had occupied the flat lands, spread their communities, built their barrows and then were lost in time and space. Their claim upon their environment was a mere sleight of hand, and yet their brief stay tells its story. It was obviously unheeded, as others claimed and continue to impose their own marks on the land, without listening to the warnings from tragedies before them.

When members of the British Empire had occupied, settled, plundered, and then sent missionaries to convert, whom had they listened to?

Forever, the cycle of man's follies returns: power, greed, ignorance, and downfall.

However, if you hear the wind in the trees and wade through the muddy stream, if you understand the sounds, sights and touch of nature, then they will speak to you, teach you, and hold you close to the mental awakening of a young child forever able to take the wrong fork and turn back, forever able to ask the question 'why' and find the true reason. Because once youth fades, the choice of turning back itself retreats from view, lost in education and occupation.

So, man's terrible persistence in following his own valued and, perhaps, calamitous route makes a weak case for loyalty and doggedness as fitting virtues: too often the same valued but flawed route is passed down, from parent to child, from authority to receiver, from the knower to the innocent, from the powerful to the weak, and from the cynical to the naïve.

But that is the story of man versus men.

But what of the story of man versus nature?

Just as the town of Maydurham sits in its own countryside cradle, so it learns from the elders that are the hills, slopes, woods and rivers. But then, the unassuming, innocent value and authority of nature is too often twisted and distorted by the malingering hand of man. Fields become cesspools, marshes become dry land and track becomes tarmac. The fowl and the beasts are tamed and dispatched, and all with the label of lucre. Husbandry befits the farmer, the shepherd, the gentle occupants of the land; they are the last ramparts between nature and the beckoning threat of mercantile wretchedness, and the unsteady and sometimes impulsive hand of power.

Man has crisscrossed the globe, trampled the plains and forests with his armies and machines and blown his own race to pieces.

His sad story is never-ending, but knowledge of the past may one day help.

* * *

The content of this story, like man's own peregrinations, wanders off the beaten track many a time. Its characters crisscross, meet and then disperse. For many, their focal point is Maydurham, a slumbering Hampshire town.

PART I

Journeymen and Rovers

Chapter 1

MARCH 1870

Henry Benjamin Harding stumbled out of his front door into the Victorian square of Concord Place. The Somerset town of Taunton, which was sculpted by riverbanks, bridges, churches, and a cricket field, was gradually waking up. Henry's door opened out onto the silk factory, which occupied one side of the square, while huddled dwellings and a cobbled street made up the rest. The air was cold, but Henry only had a five-minute walk to work. He pulled up his worn coat collar and smiled to his sister, Lydia, who watched him from the front door.

The place echoed with Henry's steps as he set off for the church of St. James, where he was working on the West Tower. His figure was rough, akin to his hands and occupation. The blasts of cold weather and the rites of the seasons had moulded him into a strong and willful stonemason, now searching for opportunities to share a livelihood with others who journeyed the country from site to site. He was still young, in his mid-twenties. His fellow stonemasons had come from Cornwall and Hampshire and plied their trade with a degree of pride. The stonework on the church and the school would provide them with further periods of employment for several months.

However, the end of winter was coming and with it thoughts about moving away.

Why remain here? Why not seek out work further east? The money seemed that way.

The thought of moving ate into Henry's spare moments, and a visit to *The Three Tuns* around the corner had led him to talking things over with Charles, another mason who lived in rooms by the silk factory. Both were committed to being independent and looked to the future to provide. Most of the families around them grew up working in the silk-factory, but Henry and Charles had turned their backs on it. Henry had already tried the loom at the age of thirteen and while he had deft hands, the experience helped him realize they were meant for stone.

The occupation of stonemason may have been harder, but Henry and Charles agreed it was their own tool bag; their mallet and chisel, the very symbols of their own authority. Tools with which to break and form their own cornerstones in life.

Nevertheless, stonemasons were bound to become journeymen, requiring a mastery of different environments to ensure their survival and success. Failure to do so, or a tainted reputation and lack of personal investment would bring their own edifice tumbling down.

Now Charles stood at the West Tower and watched Henry approach.

'So, you've been thinking about it, then?'

'What's that?'

'You know . . . leaving.'

'Keep it down, will you? We don't want everybody to

know!' Henry reminded him. 'Well, not yet, anyway. There's still plenty to do here.'

The other masons began to gather. The tower loomed above them and pierced the hazy blue early-morning sky. Pigeons flew out and scattered.

'I don't know that I would be better off elsewhere,' he continued. 'But you know what? When I was working in Wick, I met this girl. She was working in the manor house, so we got to talking, you know. She wouldn't mind moving either. Just the two of us.'

The two men stood in the yard as the sun crept over the transept roof casting their long shadows towards the gate.

'I think I'll stay put. Harriet and me, we'll probably tie the knot sometime. So, who is your lady friend?' asked Charles.

'She's called Alice. But I ain't said nothing to the folks yet. If we go, I think it'll be sudden. Guess we'll just up and go when it suits us. Dad's old, he'll find it hard, me just walking out on them like that, but when you meet somebody . . . Alice says her father walked out on them and then her mum married some man called George who she couldn't abide. So, she's got no real family. What's to stop us going? Fresh start. Some say history repeats, eh?'

Other masons had already started trimming their stones and Charles nodded towards them by the part of the tower where they had stopped at dusk the previous day.

'Best get on,' he told Henry. 'Good luck to you both.'

* * *

Alice folded the sheets and took them down the stairs to the laundry room. Later, as the air came in from the garden through the open door, she gazed at the trees lining the river. The morning was cold but bright with oaks and hazel trees clumped over the river as if harbouring the water for themselves. The whitebeams in the garden stood alone, seemingly waiting, and, for the meantime, excluded by the others. The same river drove the iron mill upstream where Alice's father had worked, where the wonderful colours mined in the hills were brought in by steam engine and turned into sheets of iron. Her stepfather had managed to find her work at the manor house, which belonged to the head of the mill. She thought it was his way of getting her out of the house.

'How strange,' she thought. 'Both of us living on the edge of industry and not really wanting to be part of it, even though it brought the people around us employment and a living.'

She turned her gaze to the stonewalled entrance to the manor, wondering what it would mean just to 'up and go' as Henry had said.

Her father had left them and walked even though he had been nothing more than a labourer. Her stepfather, George, had married her mother when Alice was five. As a result, Alice had a brother and a sister who seemed so different to her. George had never treated her as his own and her mother wanted to move on from the unhappy and wasteful time she had experienced with Alice's father. This had left Alice feeling like an uncomfortable reminder of times best forgotten.

'How do families work?' she wondered. 'Wasn't rushing off with Henry the same kind of meaningless adventure? Why was he so keen on the idea? What did he really want from her?'

Yet Alice found him interesting and his constant travel for jobs reminded her of her father. He had the same broad-set forehead and playful eyes. He had a sense of humour and a solid laugh. He also knew his own mind, but did that mean she could not share her own thoughts with him?

Would this be love or an ill-conceived relationship?

Alice plunged her hands into the cold water to scrub the sheets before setting them out to dry in the garden. Mary, the miller's daughter, passed as she returned from the garden and they nearly collided in the corridor.

'Sorry, ma'am. You nearly dropped your books!' Alice told her.

'Never mind,' the girl replied.

'You're always reading. Must be interesting. I don't seem to have a mind for reading and writing. 'Tis as much as I can do to read or write a few sentences.'

'I like books. They seem to hold me together. They have become companions. I lost so many friends when father bought the business and moved here. Are you married, Miss Alice?'

'No, but I have to say, I do think about it. You know, it's finding the right person I suppose. But then again, where you do find the right person?'

'Don't you have anybody?'

'There's a fellow from Taunton who's keen on me and says he'll carry me off to some place nice, but I don't believe him.'

The girl looked at her and remained silent.

'Yes,' Alice continued. 'I wonder if he will . . . Oh, no matter. At least you've got a book to escape into.'

Alice noticed he book cover read 'Mary Barton' by Elizabeth Gaskell and Mary saw her curiosity.

It's a very sad murder story that takes place in Manchester and Mary Barton ends up emigrating to Canada.' Mary hesitated. 'Well, I must be going'.

'Good day, ma'am,' Alice said, still intrigued, as Mary nodded to her.

She wondered if she and Henry would 'up and go' as far as that.

Chapter 2

The 'fellow from Taunton' made good his promise and carried Alice off to another world, but the reality of it was much less suited to her well-being than she thought, and their relationship soon fell apart. Roving befitted a journeyman but not a housemaid or a person in service. Henry did not aspire to settling while he was in his twenties and the nature of his job contributed to Alice's loss of employment. Furthermore, Henry's pay simply did not provide enough to keep both going.

Henry Benjamin left Alice and moved east to Hampshire where he made a new home in a rural setting with a second young woman who was also named Alice. This second Alice, Alice Maud Mary, owed her name to a spate of Alice Maud Mary christenings in the 1840s that came about through the fashion for replicating the name of Queen Victoria's third child. The princess's gentle and caring personality had endeared her to so many and her early death had brought a collective sense of grief. For thousands, christening their daughters Alice Maud Mary may have added an air of grace to their offspring, but it failed to lift them out of their precarious existence, underlining the gaping class differences and contrasting realities of Victorian Britain.

When they first moved in together, Henry and his second Alice occupied a small, whitewashed cottage in a pretty village, just a stone's throw from another St James' church. Henry was aware of the irony of his situation, the shadow of his past, and felt that he was being constantly pursued by St James.

There, briefly the new couple had been happy. The second Alice had run away from the Isle of Wight and the pair had decided to follow their stars, marrying and seeking a living in rural Hampshire. This led the stonemason and servant down a bumpy road to a village in the middle of nowhere. Stonemasonry work did not last a lifetime and Henry couldn't offer more than raucous laughter, consumption of ale, an increasingly fiery temper and little inclination to understand womankind. In another ironic twist of fate, this second Alice left Henry and returned to her roots in the Isle of Wight to marry a farm labourer.

Henry Benjamin learnt little from his relationship with either his first or his second Alice.

He moved on. The bucolic aspect of the village with its pub, fences and fields appealed, but little else captured Henry's roving imagination. Other masons had mentioned work in Portsea, so he traveled there instead, found humble lodgings and a new friend, Rose Anne, this time. She became his third wife in the first days of autumn 1877 and even on that fateful day, Henry wondered if there was any hope in their union.

He took Rose Anne to his low, heavy slated, dark, damp, and clustered working-class terrace in Finsbury Street, which left little room for happiness, but plenty of room for a sordid existence. It was all they could afford. Sailors, labourers, dockyard hands, and now a stonemason pressed themselves into semi-squalid conditions with their families. The area had been subject to cholera nearly twenty years before and conditions were still poor. Realizing the squalor of his new existence and casting about for excuses, Henry told himself he would move when work enabled him to. Later, when he had finally gone, the area was classified as 'insalubrious' and medical reports led to its clearance.

Rose Anne was so much younger than Henry. She had been in service since the age of twelve but wasn't used to the grind of this new existence with Henry. He thought they would cope but their relationship, first begun in *The Rifle,* a public house, seemed bound to fail. In the daytime Henry worked where he could and in the evening the pair of them resumed their habits at their local inn.

Then followed the dreadful fallings out, the tears, the ale swilling about in him as he bellowed at her, pushing in through the front door of their tiny abode: one room and a scullery, the yard at the back with the outdoor toilet. Rose Anne endured it for a while. At first, she had found him funny, but then the loner and drinker became all too much, and violence raised its ugly head.

After first living precariously on the edge of the slum with her parents, she had been dragged into its very midst by Henry.

With women Henry had played and lost ever since he had left home. He had eloped with Alice, his first, married Alice Maud Mary his second, and then married Rose Anne. Each couple was a failure, with the women wanting nothing more to do with him after little more than a year together.

Henry and Rose Anne's drinking provided some momentary respite but used up a good percentage of Henry's wages, leaving little to pay the rent for the squalid conditions in Finsbury Road. Eventually, even that became a quest beyond the couple's means. They moved in with Rose Anne's parents, a small dwelling and a move that only exacerbated an already venomous situation, so Henry once more picked up his stonemason's bag and set off. As he travelled onwards, he swore to himself that his moments of inebriation and loss of control should no longer affect those coming into his destructive sphere of influence. It was a bold idea, and it didn't matter if he followed through or not for he no longer had anybody and, perhaps, it was better that way.

The desire for change drove him back down to Chesil in the West where quarrying work in Portland was available and, as it was the hub of the stone industry, Henry was able to find stonemason work. He signed off as married in the census but in reality he was as a single man.

Chesil was a small rural island, sparsely inhabited, and nothing like the overcrowded and run-down slums of Portsea. Being that different, it held some form of hope. Cut by the winds and overturned by storms, Chesil backed onto St. John's church and the significance was not lost on Henry. Until then, St. James and his seeming martyrdom had followed him all the way. Maybe Henry would live as long as Saint John and write his own gospel? Was it a sign? Was he turning over a new leaf?

He decided he wasn't ready to do so and journeyed East again.

* * *

East meant Maydurham.

For the best part of twenty years, he had travelled back and forth between Somerset and various sites in Hampshire. The laborious, but above all, mind-numbing work in Portland had pushed him to follow a trail of new sites to earn a living. He needed financial independence.

The men around him often received postcards and letters from fellow journeyman stonemasons relating to work and opportunities. Henry Benjamin told them he was looking out for construction work on churches. In reply they passed on rumours relating to interesting work in Maydurham: new terraced houses and a church had been commissioned. It was a Catholic church called St Laurence's. There was news of a new post office, too. The jobs caught his interest.

The town centre offered more than enough in the way of accommodation, public houses, and inns. It had done so over the centuries to accommodate travellers on a main thoroughfare from London to the coast and it was late summer in 1889 when he found both work on a large private house and lodgings in a hotel near the station.

As the months wore on, the narrow corners of the *Sycamore Inn* became Henry's refuge. Certain companions and the occasional stranger took an interest in his trade and plans for the future. Consequently, Henry found himself gradually adapting to the rhythm of local life and the nature of Maydurham's inhabitants. The summer had been warm and easy working weather and he discovered a sense of equilibrium in his life, having been to hell and back in the slums of Portsmouth and the desolate areas of stone-cutting Portland. His origins had been modest but not akin to the type of seediness he had endured with Rose Ann in Portsea. Surely this new place signaled better days ahead.

It was on market day that Henry first encountered Louisa. Louisa's charwoman work often brought her into contact with Henry Benjamin as he finished or started his day. They regularly greeted each other, and it was in this manner that he learned about her life and children.

Louisa told Henry that she had three. A girl, Olive, going on five. A young boy, Fred, nearly three. And a six-month-old infant, Gertrude. Louisa had been a widow for just six months and was nearly thirty-two years old when they met. She was small, slim, and slight. The loss of her husband the year before had forced her to move out of her terraced house above the railway line and down into a flat in the town centre. Her husband, William, had succumbed to 'dropsy' at the age of thirty-seven whilst Louisa was pregnant with their third child. Gertrude was born forty days after William had passed on and the two other children had barely lived to know their father that well. Gertrude was delivered into the hands of a worried mother with little else but family support (her parents shared their wages with her) and an impending need to leave a dwelling she would no longer be able to pay for.

Louisa's encounters with Henry Benjamin, all swarthy features and strong frame, buoyed her up significantly, seeing that the stonemason's character had yet to reveal the undercurrents of violence and drunken behavior. For the moment, Henry's perceived sense of fun and his genuine devotion to hard work suited Louisa well enough. He was in search of a new existence and Louisa was trying to hold hers together. Their relationship grew rapidly and Louisa, living through a very anxious present, was little inclined to scrutinize his relatively sordid past. Consequently, Gertrude, although not his flesh and blood, became his first child and he became the only father she ever knew.

After a number of years, and despite the arrival of three new siblings, Henry's new Maydurham household decided that he was no longer the only father they wished to know. Alcohol, domestic violence and wasteful considerations tore into the family. The wanderer had become penned in and he proved himself incapable of dealing with the responsibilities of running a family. Ten years after their marriage Louisa and Henry were separated. In 1900 Henry Benjamin Harding was committed to the workhouse.

Droxford

Chapter 3

EARLY SPRING 1908

The winter had subsided, and the feeble but welcome watery sun was over the union workhouse. It brought a little cheer to Henry as he worked in the large kitchen garden with other inmates. The rural workhouse was not exactly daunting in terms of architecture or lifestyle. It provided safety and a livelihood, albeit limited, to those committed. That morning, Henry had been asked to sign for a new uniform. He did so and handed back the old one. *Henry Harding* was how he signed his name; Benjamin or B had gone. He was proud of his slanting elegant hand, just as he was proud of his own ability to cut and form stone. In recent weeks he had felt that he was growing old and spent time musing over his sorry fate and how he had found himself here. It was his own fault, he knew, but he was not devoid of pride or human feelings. The sad problem was – and he readily admitted it now – that drink had always been one step ahead of him.

In a very belated moment of misplaced nostalgia, he had considered writing a letter to Louisa, but his draft had been heavy-handed and although contrite, it summed up the inaccuracies of his wandering mind when it came to words and thoughts. His signature was the only expression of elegance he possessed, and he knew it. Nevertheless, his letter was sent, and he thought little of it once it was done, despite feeling somewhat better for it.

Frank, who worked next to him, sometimes tried to understand the occasional ramblings of his rough-faced dark-haired companion.

'How long have we been here now?' he asked Henry.

'I ain't really sure,' Henry answered. 'But we've definitely come down in the world. Still, at least we get on and we've got some things in common, you know, you being a brick-maker and me the stonemason.'

'Suppose so,' replied Frank. 'Except I'm a widower and you are now single. The difference is, I never knew what it was to have family. Anyway, for both of us it's a sorry state, although I have to say that life in the workhouse is easier than dealing with life outside.'

Both had been made into life's flotsam and jetsam through their own inadequacies and misfortunes.

'You know, Frank, the drink did for me good and proper. It just brought chaos into my life and had me running from one relationship to another. I was what they call a 'journeyman stonemason,' and I reckon 'journeyman' was the operative word as they say.'

Frank understood only too well; it was hardly the first time that Henry had bent his ear with his story. They shared quite a lot and being in the same trade helped.

Perhaps, Henry Benjamin had attached himself to Frank because his name reminded him of his younger brother, Francis William?

Francis had wandered a great deal further north than

him, all the way from Taunton to Yorkshire. The two brothers had never kept their ties and Henry did not know that Francis William was then dealing in horses and head of a large family.

Certainly, the absence of any family brought Henry Benjamin closer to Frank in the workhouse and opened up opportunities to share. Previously Henry had never felt the inclination to talk about his life to anyone. Now he confided in Frank, whose presence and litany of misfortunes helped him to better reflect on his inability to manage what Frank had never had and what he had lost: a family.

He knew the letter he had sent to Louisa was just an idle whim. He was no longer of an age or physique to deal with a family, and a return to any environment with a public house in his vicinity would be disastrous. Unfortunately, in Maydurham, they weren't hard to find. The main square counted four.

'You know, we could walk out of here tomorrow,' said Frank. 'It's tempting, but then this place is rather like home for me. I don't have nobody, and I am sure I'd just end up on some park bench in the middle of some town and then get taken back in anyway.'

'I'd go tomorrow, too,' replied Henry. 'But that seems to be my problem. I've spent my life moving on and then losing out somehow. I left Taunton for Alice and that came to nothing. Then I met another Alice, and that was a failure. I married Rose Anne and then that never worked out and then I married Louisa, but each time it was the drink that ate into me.'

'You know, when I think of the dives I have been in

before, this is probably the first decent place I've actually wanted to stay in. It's a fair change, I must say,' Frank said repeating what he had already said. It was his turn to go over one of their ritual themes.

The sun pulled out from behind a cloud and lit up the front yard of the workhouse. Henry stopped digging, stuck the spade in the ground and turned to Frank.

'You know, I think when I was with Rose Anne, I had my head in some kind of vice,' he said, unaware of the pun. 'I couldn't think for myself or for us. Portsmouth was like being stuck in the worst living conditions you can imagine, and Rose wanted something different. She thought we could go and live in the Isle of Wight. So, to keep her happy, some days we'd walk up on to Portsdown and look at the island in the distance, then we saw Buckland and wondered how we ever got there.'

'Like I said, this place has its virtue,' Frank responded.

'Yeah. So, what's tomorrow made of? Going nowhere, I suppose.' He paused. 'By the way, I've written to Louisa.'

'What for? She's never going to take you back after all this time and the locals won't want you,' asked Frank.

'You have a point,' Henry replied.

He rubbed his hands together and turned them over, they were still worn and calloused with the use of stone, hammers and chisels, and reminded him of that awful afternoon some eight years ago.

* * *

Those same hands struggled to hold on to the heavy rosette-shaped door knocker, caught their fingers in the letter box, then slid down the wall of Dog Alley as he tried to catch his balance.

'Louisa,' he shouted.

He stood again and grappled with the doorknocker and banged loudly, shouting for Louisa to open it.

Louisa had already left to clean for a big house near the lake. Would she have let him in anyway?

'Louisa!' he groaned. 'Open the bloody door!'

It would hardly have been the first time that Henry had stumbled in, inebriated and loud, attempting to manhandle Louisa before sinking into a chair.

'Help, Louisa!'

The spring afternoon sun reflected off the large windows of the bank opposite and blinded Henry as he turned trying to see if any passers-by were watching. The glare was bright and overpowering. His face felt rough, his head was awry with the roll of dizziness and he stretched out his arms again to grip the door handle.

'Bloody women,' he uttered and lay on his side trying to regain part of his senses, in vain.

He had spent his pay on this. That much he knew.

Looking out into the street he caught the reverberation of the sun's glare once more before it was blotted out by a dark human form.

'Are you all right, sir?'

'Uh,' Henry replied tentatively, realising that someone was attempting to engage in a dialogue with him.

The man knelt beside him and repeated his question.

'Are you all right, sir? It looks like you've had one too many.'

Henry saw there was a chain running from the man's breast pocket to a button of his jacket.

'Perhaps, you ought to come with me.'

With assistance Henry stood, and the other man helped him back out into the street.

They made their way slowly past the square and the church and entered a low flint- and stone-walled building.

Another man came to the door and they both helped Henry into a small room off the yard at the back.

As they closed the door on him, the man with the chain said:

'Drunk in Dog Alley at three fifteen pm.'

'Thank you, Constable. I will put him in for the petty sessions. Remanded until Friday.'

'The family needs to be alerted. Apparently, nobody was in. At least when I picked him up. I'll go back later this afternoon.'

Remanded, thought Henry. I'm being remanded.

Henry's prison cell picked up the voices and conversations of those descending the alleyway behind the police station, as well as the chime of the church bell, and the occasional rumbling of a motor vehicle. Birds on the great sycamore in the churchyard sang their spring song while Henry sat on his bench in silent attendance. The effects of the drink were gradually draining out of him, confirmed by the level of the bucket in the corner. A sense of regret rose and pressed in on him. Although he was only one foot from the daily routines of passers-by on the other side of the wall, he was paradoxically now much nearer to a lengthy exclusion from his usual environment.

The journeyman never ceases to journey but sadly and

for too long Henry had been moved on by his own dark forces and the side-effects of his own misjudgments and mistakes, in stark contrast to the epitome of the stonemason who wields the hammer and chisel, usually the symbols of mastery and authority. And now the same person, in the simple role of a husband and father, had continued to confound and incur disproportionate damage on those closest to him.

He was remanded, and, if his case of incapacity to maintain a family and recurrent inebriation were confirmed, he would be destined for prison and hard labour. Louisa never came for him, neither that evening nor the next morning. The police went to her and collected his belongings instead. Although his own three children aged nine, six and three were confused, his three step-children had a clearer idea of the ordeal.

Henry sat and occasionally lay in his cell that night, unaware that all of the talk was between Louisa, Olive, and the Constable, hardly suspecting that from this very moment on he would be severed from his family.

In the coming times, he would know nothing of the remarkable workings of the matriarchy of Olive, Louisa, and later Gertrude who gradually asked and answered the right questions, while Fred set about making a living for himself and the family. They all saw survival as their goal: work, pay the rent, and save what they could. And they stuck to it: there was no alternative. Choices between pride or shame, occupation or idleness, community or exclusion were obvious. Love and protection were their watchwords.

The same choices and watchwords could have been

negotiated and heeded by Henry; he could have kept the family afloat and relatively happy, but he didn't.

Henry sensed that from the outset, almost as an intruder, he had broken into a stronger group than he had expected, and despite his journeying, bouts of drinking and violence, his own children with Louisa were now protected and sheltered from his own misdemeanours thanks to the common sense, love and the commitment of a mother and elder children bound together to outlive his poisonous paternal presence.

As the afternoon turned into evening, he ruminated over how he had engineered his own banishment from his offspring and wife.

Or was there more to it than that? What had driven him to spend his life wandering, drinking and failing miserably in his relationships with women? Had it been a family trait?

Footsteps stopped at the door and a plate was handed to him.

'The hearing in the courthouse will take place tomorrow,' he learnt as the evening gloom descended.

'My wife and children?' he asked.

'We've seen them, and they know you are here.'

He ate and the sun finally set on the other side of the church. He drifted off to sleep before he had had time to answer his own questions.

The next day's session led to Henry being taken into custody once he had admitted to neglecting to maintain his wife and family. Consequently, he would soon appear before the local magistrate, the Poor House Union Guardian, the constable who had picked him up, and the solicitor's clerk.

* * *

The small flint walled courthouse could hardly have held more than those few persons. Henry sat in the tiny box reserved for the defendants and looked through the high windows facing north. The clear April sky beckoned. He listened as PC Sealey described how he had picked up Mr. Henry Benjamin Harding and how the latter had pleaded guilty to being 'drunk and disorderly' when remanded in custody.

The local magistrate ran through the details and pronounced:

'Members of this hearing, it is proved thus, beyond any doubt, that Henry Benjamin Harding is chargeable with regards to the neglect of his three offspring, step-children and wife.'

Henry stood, felt the iron handcuffs tug his hands down his back, exited the miniature courtroom, saw the blue sky beckon again and found himself mounting the steps into the carriage with the constable.

The 25th April 1900 he was convicted and sentenced to six week's imprisonment and hard labour for being drunk and disorderly and neglecting the maintenance of his family despite his proven means. The Poor House Union then took him in and relieved the family once and for all of their burden.

* * *

Henry finished the row he was digging then retreated to the courtyard at the front of the workhouse, running the pictures through his mind once more. This time he knew there was no going back, despite his awkward letter. It had been more than eight years since that day. He was fairly sure that Louisa and the children could only have been better off without him. After all, through the little he had learnt about them, they had settled into a routine that was a great deal more peaceful than that of the upheavals he had brought upon them with his fitful journeying for work and capacity to drink his wages away.

'Six weeks of prison and hard labour, then the Workhouse,' he muttered to himself. 'Eight years in the Workhouse. The sentence was about right.'

Frank heard him.

'Yes, it's our lot,' he said.

The inmates filed inside, and the large kitchen garden stood empty. All had finished their jobs and the watery sunshine had slunk away from the fields.

The workhouse grounds overlooked a country road, adorning a placid and benevolent-looking front. Gravel paths, trees and flowerbeds accompanied the visitor in. Once inside, you would see it was divided into special segments: a hexagonal building with six spokes or passageways and six triangular courtyards in its midst, there to divide and separate the different inmates.

The inmate could come and go as he wished but leaving without requesting his own effects and still wearing the regulation uniform meant he was also leaving with stolen goods on his back, which was a chargeable offence.

The front doors stood open and the last light from the South West lit up the master's office. Despite the temptation and a new outfit Henry knew he would probably be going nowhere. Soon it would be nightfall, closure on another day. Henry found it hard to deny that at sixty-two years old, the lifestyle afforded by the rural workhouse was reasonable and accepted that his family had probably forgotten about him.

Maydurham

Chapter 4

SPRING 1908

'I'll be twenty next October.'

Gertrude said goodbye to her mother, exited Dog Alley, and turned towards the square.

She was heading for the large boarding house run by the two elderly sisters because they were in need of permanent help and she was in need of a job. They had offered her lodgings, a room with a view over the fields, which was tempting because it eased the congestion in the flat above the shop in the High Street where she had lived with her mother and siblings.

She passed the old Joliffe workhouse, reminding her of her stepfather, Henry Benjamin Harding and his destiny some fifteen miles away. Gertrude was of slight build like her mother with an angular face and a mop of uncontrollable wiry hair. As an adolescent her dark-eyed look seemed to challenge you and her stride was regular. She could daydream too though. Perhaps the result of a complex childhood.

Being that Gertrude's own father had died before she had been born and her stepfather Henry had been beyond the pale, she wondered if any men on this earth were beholden to, or even supported their family. The time she spent with her younger siblings and half-siblings gave her much joy and she was very close to Mabel or 'May' as her mother called her, and Rose. Her older sister, Olive, kept watch. May spent her time with the cats and Rose reminded her of herself; ever the gangly girl who was readier for fun and carried an eternal spark in her eye. Sadly, Rose's underlying health problems would thwart her ambitions and relationships.

'Twenty.'

She smiled and mused at the mischief, which seemed to take over her heart whenever she fell in with people. Her boyish looks and forthright sense of fun meant she was always in high spirits when with friends. Even as a child she seemed to be made for moving on and taking people with her: nature's child, free in spirit, body and mind. Perhaps, that was what attracted her young man, Charles. Her older brother, Fred, was just the same. He studied animals and spent his time reading comic books, sharing them with her. They were close and never short of ideas. Fred said he would tame lions and work in a circus, but later ran errands, delivered the post and sold newspapers. Gertrude never really knew if she could tame lions but enjoyed escaping the cage of her small-town existence with her mother and older sister, Olive, in Portsmouth at the shops; at least, on occasional afternoons. The train ride and the thought of the seaside pleased her. Olive, too, was good for everybody. She held her head like a lady and probably would have been, if she hadn't been in service.

Just weeks after the death of Queen Victoria in 1901, when she was twelve, they went to Blair's *Crystal Palace*

Studio for their photo. Mr. Blair placed Olive to the back; she was the tallest, the most elegant – the elder to look after her care-worn mother sitting in front her with baby William adorning the black ribbon on her knees. Her mother had borne six infants and Olive had been the first. Gertrude reckoned that Olive had probably taken on at least ten years of sisterly care for five siblings, first deprived of one father and then of another. Both husbands, Frederick and then Henry, had spent only a decade each with their wife and families. Olive had become a second mother to the younger children while Gertrude and Fred's roles were more akin to that expected of siblings; love, fun and just enjoying growing up together.

Gertrude liked Mr. Blair. He was good to the locals and knew how to bring the best out of a group. His photos all seemed natural. Blair took more than a family snapshot, something leaning towards the classic portrait but without going the whole way. With Louisa's family it was not easy to strike a classical or formal tone. Gertrude knew her irreverent pose bore witness to just that and her hair, like Rose's, was impossible to manage; just one symbol of the energy that radiated amongst the children. During the session Gertrude looked wide-eyed, earnestly and questioningly, almost insolently, at the camera. Olive was dignified. Little Mabel looked surprised. Fred posed naturally. Louisa looked for answers much in the same way as Gertrude. Rose contained a smile and infant Bill was following the looks beyond Mr. Blair to the rear of the room where he kept two cats, one of which was now held by Mabel. Three looks concentrated on Mr. Blair's black box, three slightly off to the left of the camera and Gertrude's was neither.

Several days later, when they had received the print, Louisa observed the group and wondered what Gertrude could have been thinking about. She concluded that her daughter must have found the whole photographic rigmarole tedious.

By now both elder daughters had been in service for several years, Rose had started out more recently. May would shun service for embroidery.

Gertrude reached the narrow road leading to the large house set in the field. Just on the other side of the road an empty bench looked up at the South Downs.

As she entered, Lily Alice the housekeeper, held out a postcard.

'Your young man.'

Gertrude blushed and took the card.

She had met Charlie three years ago when he had been stationed in Bordean. Coming into town one clear spring evening with the other soldiers, he had sat in the square while the curious townsfolk shared conversations with the group. Gertrude had stood by. One of the groups had engaged her brother in conversation. They had seemed to find common ground.

'So, you play in a band?' said Fred. 'Well so do I! In fact, I started it a few years ago. I play brass instruments.'

'I'm a drummer,' said the soldier. 'What stuff do you play?'

Their conversation was caught up in the general brouhaha and Gertrude was unable to hear the rest but knew the answers. She realized she had caught the soldiers' glances. She was pretty. Her curls hung around her face. She gazed with curiosity and innocence at this sudden arrival of uniforms; the uniforms elevated all and sundry to another rank in life and inspired respect.

When Fred turned to another soldier, she found herself face to face with the young bandsman and his dark features.

'Are you brother and sister?' asked the soldier.

'Yes,' she replied with a smile.

'You come from here, too?'

'Yes, we live in the town. Fred works at the newsagents and I just started in service.'

'Big family. There are five of us. My brothers are in the army, too.'

It occurred to Gertrude once again that Fred was the only male in the family doing a job and pulling his weight, what with father dead and the stepfather in the workhouse.

One day while she was in the sweet shop next to Dog Alley, a neighbour had told her that her brother would be a genuine *polymath*. So, she went to the library to ask the meaning.

'A bit of a Jack-of-all-trades,' the librarian had told her. The librarian's description was right: her brother took on all sorts of jobs because he was planning for the future.

Gertrude, herself, was curious and able. She'd learned well at the girls' school and carried a head on her shoulders so to speak, enabling her to manage the money she earned. She had common sense in abundance, despite the wistful and mischievous looks she sometimes gave. But as with so many women of her time, she wasn't always able to have the last word where men were concerned.

The young soldier had a tall youthful and wiry frame, dark eyebrows and a smart moustache. Moustaches were the fashion. He was soft spoken and took an interest in Gertrude's contrasting ebullience.

'What's your name?'

'Charlie, Charlie Soloman, but the lads call me 'Sammy'.'

'And you?'

'Gertrude.'

'See you next time we're in town?'

Gertrude nodded.

The soldiers, a confident bunch, moved off to the railway station. Fred and his sister carried the remaining papers back to the shop.

* * *

'Your young man? Good news, I hope?' Lily Alice asked again and roused Gertrude from her reverie when she had finished the card.

'Yes, Miss. He says he'll be back in Hampshire in September.'

'And I'll be twenty in October. My life's just about to begin.'

She put the postcard in her bag and hurried to the scullery where she enjoyed baking cakes for the residents of the boarding house. Charles and Gertrude had first met in 1905 and he wrote at every opportunity when he was travelling around the world with the army and, better still, paid her a visit whenever he was garrisoned in the vicinity.

Chapter 5

Olive, unlike her sister, was involved in a more sedate romance which was in keeping with her own own nature, serious and practical-minded. She closed the door of the large house and set off for her mother's rooms over the shop. The spring leaves on the towering elms shut out the sunlight and turned the Avenue into an unkempt mottled tunnel with hints of brick grey at one end and dark fir green and blue at the other. The blur of colours reminded her of those in the Turner print placed over the fireplace.

Olive was the only child to have clear memories of their father. Fred was barely two when he died. Gertrude wasn't even born then. Although Olive was only four when he passed on, she had images of his angular features with dark hair, a pointed nose and pointed chin. And despite being a labourer, he bore no hallmarks of excessive strength and got by with a lean and wiry frame. Olive often thought that Gertrude's young man probably looked something like the father they hardly knew.

Ever since their mother, Louisa, had moved to the flat after William's death, their lives had become precarious. However, living above the shop in the centre of town meant that news and rumours for potential work and contacts abounded just below them. Louisa had cleaned for the townsfolk while her first husband, William, had toiled in the fields. The farming community thrived on the edge of the town. Varieties of cereals, cattle and even hops for the brewery supplied employment. Both had made a living. Nevertheless, after William's early death, her second marriage had gradually become a worrisome and different story. Olive surmised that her mother had just jumped at an opportunity to secure a husband for family support. Henry Benjamin Harding, the journeyman stonemason, was looking for lodgings and one thing led to another.

Gertrude and Olive followed similar working lives to their mother's own. Both were in service in houses run by a pair of elderly sisters, albeit at both extremities of the town. Gertrude's was a boarding house whereas Olive's was a large private house named 'Cossington'. The Campbell sisters who lived there and employed Olive were from Australia. They also employed a Belgian girl, so Olive felt that she had a privileged and broader vision of life. The large gabled house sat back from the corner of the road and housed beautiful paintings and different ornaments from around the world. Olive's eyes were constantly drawn to the beautiful blue and yellow Chinese vase adorned with magpies and wisteria and the prints in the entrance hall, which had been taken after the Boxer Rebellion. The sisters said they had been 'plundered' before coming into their possession.

The sisters also spoke at length about history. When their friends came, Olive noticed that they often sat round the drawing room table discussing the latest newspaper reports, which covered the progress of the Suffragettes. Both Olive and Gertrude had recently met someone. Olive had become acquainted with Tom who was in the Royal Navy and now her curiosity led her to spend her moments of distraction in front of a print of one of Turner's paintings. Previously her thoughts about the sea had been confined to the shingle on Southsea front and the movement of the different craft. Now with a young man in the Navy, the picture challenged her to formulate ideas about the pride and history of the senior service and its place in the artistic world.

At first, it had seemed to her a wonderful display of colours. But as she stood before it now, the *Fighting Temeraire Tugged to Her Last Berth to Be Broken up* seemed like a ghost being dragged out of the past by the awful wafting smoke and industrial form of the dark and blackened tug. The glorious vessel of the Battle of Trafalgar was hardly able to force herself on to the canvas and Olive bent to check the detail which faded before her eyes. Another great sailing ship hung back in the distance, also part of another time.

Then, by comparison, she imagined the black and billowing funnels of the *Dreadnought* and Tom standing splendidly on the deck on his way out of port. But the colours were far from those of those that Turner had worked into his picture. She could only picture the pale blue sky and the colossal grey forms of the towers and turrets as the low-lying battlecruiser slipped away.

For the moment this was Olive's secret and her sensible nature dictated that she would only let others know when the right time came. Gertrude was the only person who suspected her sister had her eyes on a young service man whose regular absences also allayed any suspicions.

As she approached the shop Mabel and William appeared at the exit to Dog Alley.

'Mum's had some news. It's not good. Father's written and he maybe they'll let him out,' said Mabel.

Olive halted in her tracks and the blood ran from her

cheeks. Under no circumstances could she or the family conceive of more upheaval or violence re-entering their lives.

She was adamant: 'Well, he can't come here, and he'll be made unwelcome, if he makes any attempt. People around here know too well about him and his habits and I shouldn't expect the farms or builders offering work.'

Reassured, Mabel turned to a blank-looking William.

'So, you see, perhaps we don't have to worry after all.'

Nevertheless, Mabel worried for William; she was already making plans for herself, but William was still at school. If father were to come back, then William would be alone with his mother to deal with him and he was still only eleven.

At the age of fourteen Mabel had started dressmaking at the local milliners-cum-drapers and found herself absorbed in ideas of patterns and sizes. She loved working with ribbons and bows. It wasn't much, but what could young women do? The choices were limited to shopkeeping, dressmaking, domestic service and the unthinkable. Fortunately, plenty of the established households called into the draper's shop for all varieties of clothes and hats: that sufficed for the time being. The family had to make ends meet with virtually five of the six siblings and the mother all playing their part.

'Yes, but Mum's worried sick he'll come back,' Mabel added suddenly.

Olive turned into the alleyway, opened the door and mounted the stairs. Louisa was pleased to see her elder daughter.

'He's written to tell me he wants to come back and find work. I don't want him back.'

'I know, mother, I've just seen May and Bill. Look, mum, there's no place for him and the local constabulary know that he won't be able to account for himself here. How many times did they pick him up in the streets? Do you remember how he treated us? There is no way they will let him back. They can't.'

Louisa continued to wear the anxious look that had descended on her several years ago; smiling no longer seemed part of her ritual. Her looks so contrasted with the rounder and fuller face and equanimous-looking forehead of her daughter. Olive's life, so far, had been simpler, despite the loss of her father and the whirlwind relationship with her stepfather with whom she had shared few interests or habits.

The two women looked at each other and Louisa felt her pride in Olive rise. Her daughter had cared for all of them in just as many ways as Louisa had tried. She had applied greater strength and energy to handle the ordeals of the drunken and violent father and cared for the smaller ones when there were just not enough hands to go around. She had also brought a little money into the household through her domestic service.

It was as if all these women could do now was to make up for the time taken from them by death and the ravages of alcoholism. Their lives had only one aim: to survive and enjoy what they may. Life for the boys would work out. It was still very much a man's world.

Mabel's full round face pressed in at the door as Bill hung back at the top of the stairs. Her eyes wore a pointed look and her nose looked like a button from one her dress-making boxes.

'So, what do we do?' she asked.

'Nothing,' replied Olive. 'He won't be back, and he knows full well he can't come back. He's not welcome in this household nor in this town.'

Chapter 6

A number days later and some fifty yards away from Louisa's flat, William Lyndsey Halden was getting his pub ready for opening time. Shading his eyes, he saw the sun illuminate the outline of the church and the trees opposite. The marketplace filled with light and farmers. He opened the main door and the sun caught him head on. The sun of Maydurham, the same sun as that of Cannes where he had grown up. The same sun of the Devon farm where he had helped his grandfather while he was just a young scholar. The same sun that had watched over the last breath of his younger sister, Anne Catherine, and his despairing parents before the darkness of their having to register her death and plan her burial in France.

But France was the sunshine. His parents had moved out of Broadclyst to work at the *Château Sainte Anne*. The new wealthy British gentry needed villas, gardens and staff. His father's gardening credentials recognized by the established families of Devon had given him a stepping stone into the world of the eminently rich in the south of France. The gardens of the villa bore witness to William Lyndsey's first steps and his infancy in quarters occupied by his parents and other servants. Later he scampered down the steps, crunched the broad gravel paths and played on the four great grass rectangles before pulling at his father's sleeves and trousers as he worked on the tall luxuriant shrubs running around the edges of the plot. The blue of the Mediterranean was visible from the terrace and the heat was everywhere.

William Lyndsey, his brothers and sisters had all been born and had grown up in large new plots of the rich and wealthy on the French Riviera. They had come back to England with another sense of well-being under their skin, but knew it was out of their reach. The walks into the hills behind the villa and the descent to the sea on the *Croisette* were long gone but William Lyndsey could still feel the experience in his bones.

He cast his mind back to the day when the passenger ship had docked in Southampton and he had walked down the gang plank under the grey overcast skies to catch the train bearing him back to Exeter. Next came further schooling, work on the farm and a move to Hampshire, first as manager of a small general store and then a licensee of the public house right in the middle of the town. But now his dandy looks were gradually declining, confirmed by the redness in his puffy face when last orders were called, and the day drew to a close.

Ada stood behind him and cast her eyes on the market square.

'Back in France again?' She asked.

'Nearly.'

'Well, it won't get this place working, just dwelling on the past.'

'I know. But thinking about it does . . .'

'Does what?'

'Tempt me.'

'You mean, going back?' she interrupted.

'Would you like to live there?' William suggested.

'I don't speak the language.'

Ada picked up the broom and started on the wooden floor. William turned his attention to the work in the back-room. With the barrels and bottles. Their touch had already awakened the ache in his mind and the feeling that he no longer wanted to cope. That there was something better to do.

Their son, William Henry, was a ship's boy, returning irregularly from his different voyages no more than an able seaman but with more than satisfactory reports on most of his ship records. Maybe, he had inherited his father's wanderlust. He was their only child.

William Lyndsey Halden left the doorstep to watch as the brewer's men fitted new equipment in the backyard. Ada appeared at the door ready to deal with the first customers, so, considering he had a little free time, he crossed the square and walked towards the tobacconist's.

Devon, Broadclyst, and Exeter had always consumed his memories, not so much for his few years there, but more for trying to understand why his parents had suddenly uprooted themselves and left for France.

Had his father felt that he had grown up in the middle of nowhere?

Surely the cottage in the fields had been a bucolic, although remote, form of existence. It also allowed contact with the landed gentry and had enabled his father to first cut his cloth as a gardener, and as time progressed, as an established gardener and landscaper.

Different reasons came to mind.

There was the cholera that had come in from the ports

and added to the pressure on families to re-locate or cast about for safety elsewhere. There was also the account that his father had encountered Sir Thomas Acland after church one Sunday. Acland's brother had written a pamphlet about the well-being of the climate of Cannes for sufferers of tuberculosis. The British aristocracy were on the move and Sir Thomas Acland might well have believed that he was advancing both his own cause and that of that William Halden senior, whose serious landscaping credentials would certainly help his wealthy connections bound for the South of France.

William remembered the lush plants and the gentle climate at the *Chateau Sainte Anne* he had first opened his eyes to. Recalling the privileged slopes of the *boulevard d'Oxford* in Cannes, he could still hear the sound of wheelbarrows on the gravel paths, the sight of water cascading from the lion-headed gargoyle into the shell-shaped basins, which then overflowed from one into another, and finally formed a stream running to the bottom of the garden.

He loved the palm trees, planted to decorate, to provide shade and break up the lines of stone walls and ponds, and to camouflage the *jardin potager* where he and his sister Alice hid and watched the unceasing activity of the gardeners and builders as they raised high stone walls above the beautiful arched arbours that encouraged the onlooker to come and while away the time in the company of large potted cacti and bougainvillea.

His father had benefited from a Victorian period of wealth, expansion, and subsequent investment in sunnier climes. Gardeners were needed, found and dispatched to complete the Mediterranean's new resorts where earls, dukes and even future kings found time for leisure, banquets, garden parties and politicking.

Several years ago, his father had passed him an old newspaper cutting of the Prince of Wales' 1894 visit to *Sainte Anne's* for a spring garden party.

> The splendid gardens were greatly admired . . . the new rooms are magnificent, and the grounds are extensive and perfectly kept. There is a lake of moderate dimensions, hundreds of orange trees, palms, bamboos etc., are distributed about the tastefully laid-out grounds.

His father had chuckled.

'Must say I'm pretty chuffed to have been part of the beginning of *Sainte Anne's*, but we didn't put the lake in. Captain Vyner's men must have done it,' he said.

William had kept the cutting and had always felt the need to return to Sainte Anne's one day.

But that warm and optimistic time had now passed them all by. His parents were back and living in the countryside nearby. His sister Alice had come back, too, but they saw little of each other. Alice travelled, buying and selling dress materials from France. Anne Catherine had died in France barely four years old, and his other siblings Elizabeth, John Robert and Henry had all departed this world when back in England. They hadn't been able to reach the turn of the century, thus replicating the sad common denominator that required a family to provide many children to enable a few to survive. His father had come from a family of ten.

He had come from a family of six. Now he had just one

son and a wife. Family planning had changed, but then so had his lifestyle, compared to that of his ancestors, who had been of solid West Country stock until Cannes. Now he lived over the town square, just a few seconds from the tobacconist's whose proprietor stood empty-handed in front of him as William awoke from his revery.

'Day-dreaming, William?' asked Mr. Rowswell.

'Sorry, miles away, you know. How's the wife?'

'She's fine. Upstairs with Louisa. Apparently, her former husband, Henry, has written.'

William had been made aware of the difficult saga in Louisa's household years ago through the gossip infiltrating his public house. Henry Benjamin's roving and trails of disaster in the West Country and Hampshire had contrasted considerably with his own experience of growing up in France and his later journey to England. He never related this comparison to Ada who generally ruminated over the stories that emerged in the pub, because she thought that a little knowledge gained here and there could be of use either in helping some people and in avoiding others.

'Well, I hope we won't have to start picking him out of the gutter once more,' William remarked.

'Poor fellow. They say he's in Droxford Workhouse now. He's getting closer.'

'That I wouldn't know,' said William.

William returned to his pub and helped the men carry the old parts of the pumps and pipes to their cart. He was proud of his business, it was far more responsibility than he had ever experienced, but along with it came the anxiety of making things a relative success. His fine blue-eyed oval face, his gently sophisticated features and his continental past had brought out the gentleman, especially when he wore his bowler hat, pinned tie and riding jacket. But he was approaching forty and his looks were beginning to suffer from furrows and folds in his brow, and crows' feet had appeared around his eyes.

Ada also provided him with pressure. The ex-schoolmistress was organized and expected the same of her husband: running the pub did not allow time for drifting off and reminiscing, and she often told him as much. She had come from a family of tradespeople and progressing in life was her byword. The one thing she regretted was the absence of numerous children. William Henry was her only son. He had helped and had been willing, still only fourteen, but did not seem interested in running a pub. The navy had inspired him, and he had been keen to enlist, so there would be nobody to take over the business.

William reappeared at the door to the pub and nodded to Ada.

'I have just been to Rowswell's. Did you know that Henry Harding's written to Louisa?' he told her.

'He's the last person she needs,' she replied scornfully.

'I daresay. Funny how some just leave trails of disaster in their wake. What was that expression? You know, 'strait is the gate'?'

'Something to do with going to heaven through a narrow door, and if you don't get yourself organized there'll be no customers wanting to come through that door,' replied Ada.

PART 2

The Blood of Eden

Maydurham

Chapter 7

OCTOBER 1908

Gertrude was waiting for Charles at the station. He had visited regularly when billeted locally. For three years they had spent time together irregularly and corresponded mainly through postcards. The more recent were signed off with kisses and love. He had been on army exercises in Wales and was later heading for Dublin, and whenever he was able to return, they spent time in the confines of the house where Gertrude was working or where her friends could provide sanctuary. Visibly he bore the status of Gertrude's young man, but the fitful nature of their relationship irked both Louisa and Olive. Louisa worried for her daughter after the loss of her two husbands and wanted nothing less than an enduring and reliable relationship for her.

Gertrude's relationship with her soldier was under scrutiny.

She was the first to court earnestly. Despite the difference in age, she had met a likely suitor well before Olive, but Olive looked more rationally at men's hearts. Gertrude had the spark and carefree nature to set against her stock of common sense. It was a question of which would gain the upper hand.

As she stood at the entrance to the station, travellers filtered out and Charles appeared with a heavy bag. He put it down.

He folded her into his army greatcoat, and they held on to each other, silently.

'Twenty! Happy Birthday. This is for you.' Charles handed her a little parcel. 'Did you miss me?' he asked.

'Thanks. Did *you* miss me?' she asked.

'Of course, did you get my letter?'

'Yes, it was lovely. So, you're going to Ireland?'

'Yes, we'll be there in November. That's for sure,' he replied.

'Is Frank going with you?'

'Yes.'

Frank and Charles were army friends and travelling companions. They always took off together when on furlough. This time he hadn't come. Gertrude and Charles were alone. It was her birthday, the 11th October 1908.

They walked down from the station into the town square where Charles invited her into a pub. She sat near the window opposite the bar. Charles fetched the drinks. The landlord nodded to her.

'Hello, Mr. Halden.'

'Hello, Gertrude, how's your mum?'

'Well, if it weren't for our stepfather pestering her, she would have had less to worry about.'

William Halden was relieved that Henry Benjamin Harding's drinking bouts had not taken place on his watch and in his public house.

Charles returned with the drinks.

'Your young man, Gertrude?'

Gertrude blushed and nodded.

'Where are you from, sir?' asked William.

'Well, my family's in Sussex but we come up from Devon way.'

'You don't say. So, does ours. Around Broadclyst. It's a remote part of the world.'

'We're from up north in Tiverton.' Charles added.

'Nice place, too.'

Gertrude thought that these types of encounters enabled pieces of puzzles to fall into place or seemed to have some kind of meaning. William returned to his work. She held the little package Charles had given her.

'What is it?' Gertrude asked.

'Open it. You'll see. Happy Birthday!'

She found a kidney-shaped locket on a necklace with nothing inside.

'It's pretty. Thank you, Charlie. What shall I put in it? A photo?'

'One of me, I hope.'

'Are you off to Dublin soon? I mean, this week?'

'Yes, we'll be in Pembroke on Monday.'

'You must have been round the world with all the traveling you do.'

'Well . . . only South Africa really. That's the furthest.'

They stood up to leave. William watched them go and wondered about their difference in age.

Most of the Kimble-Hardings have yet to reach adulthood, he thought .

When the couple arrived at Gertrude's boarding house, they found themselves alone and the couple went to Gertrude's room.

He took her in his arms.

Their desperation to catch up the time they hadn't spent together left them breathless. But there was also awkwardness in their impatience as it overtook them.

How were they to control the rashness of young lovers? Gertrude asked herself.

Charles was nearly eight years older than Gertrude. He was her first man. She wasn't his first woman. What did *she* really know about lovemaking?

Their nakedness was her joy and embarrassment. Her nakedness was his joy with no embarrassment. The roles of men and women seemed predestined only to be scrutinized and dissected by all. The age of shame hung heavily in many families.

She gathered up her clothes and they sat together laughing. She asked when he would settle down and if the army was to be his lifetime pursuit. He spoke about his brothers also in the army and how soldiering now seemed to run in the family's blood. Gertrude thought that if he had said it another way, she would have been terrified. He laughed again and said he was proud to be in *The Rifles*.

That evening they returned to the station and held on to each other before Charles left for Dublin.

* * *

A few weeks later Gertrude found herself gazing out of the same window on to the pastures leading to the downs. The trees on the skyline had taken on the heavy hues of autumn. The cold was increasingly perceptible, and the damp leaves gathered in the ditches. The road sweepers worked their way down the lane helping the runnels to flow. Another season would soon roll by, but Gertrude had the feeling that things were not right. She fingered the locket that hung around her neck.

Chapter 8

Christmas and winter closed in on the town. The temperatures were dropping, and people stopped draughts whistling under their doors wherever they could.

Thinking she would light a fire, Louisa readied the hearth and cleared some family photos from the mantlepiece in her flat above the shop. Looking at them, she wondered how she and the children had survived the disappearance of two men. Work had been her only way out. As a charwoman at least she had found the opportunities to do extra work for special occasions or had been able to find work for her daughters. Her son, Fred, was different. He somehow knew where he was going before any of the family had. His ability to carry out errands, find odd jobs, involve himself with local tradesmen meant he was constantly occupied. Bill was coming twelve and still at school. His looks reminded her so much of Henry.

At fifty-one she was beginning to find her job increasingly challenging and was hoping they could move out of the town to a house with a little garden where she could occasionally put her feet up in the sunshine. The flat was dark inside, even in the summer days. Another Christmas and the prospect of snow and slush would add a new dimension to moving around the town.

As she looked at the solemn and solid architecture of the

bank opposite, the front door was opened, and Gertrude came in.

'You're just in time for tea,' Louisa said.

'Thanks, Mum.'

Gertrude looked around as if searching for a stage cue and stopped at the mantlepiece where she had been accustomed to seeing the family photos.

'Did you take the photos down?' she asked her mother.

'Yes, I wanted to put them in the album to stop them getting dusty.'

'Oh, so what will you put in their place?'

'A nice mirror . . . I was just going to light the fire.'

Gertrude thought about how she could have cast an eye over her own looks, if there had been a mirror there before. Now the thought of the mirror left her cold.

'Mother. I have to tell you something.'

'Is it anything upsetting?'

'Erm, well . . .'

'I hope not.'

'I don't know, Mum, but I think I am expecting.'

'Sorry, Gertie, did I hear you right? You're expecting a child? Are you sure?'

Gertrude paused.

'It's been nearly two months.'

Louisa held on to the door frame and looked at her daughter. Everything she had planned or dreamed for herself had come second to what the men in her life had wanted. Was her own daughter to find herself in the same predicament? Were events supposed to overtake you before you could even hope to organize life? Or was it just a woman's lot? She knew the moment was of tremendous weight for both of them and above all she knew the happy heart of her daughter had been plunged into disarray.

'Is it your soldier friend?'

'Yes.'

'Does he know?'

'No. Not yet. I am going to write. He's in Dublin.'

'Oh, Gertie. I don't know what to say. Look at me. I have had six of you and I started when I was twenty-seven and you're still a slip of a girl. You're barely twenty.'

'You don't have to tell me, mother.'

'Does anybody know . . . apart from us two?'

'I don't think so, but Misses Annie and Mary know that I have been seeing Charlie. They've always lent him a sympathetic ear.'

'So, what about your job, then? They're good people,' said Louisa. 'They have always looked after you. Perhaps, you should tell them. They will probably doubt something later on, given the time you spend there. That is, if you don't intend to leave. Anyway, you will have to tell them.'

Gertrude considered it and seemed to find consolation in the idea of speaking to her employers.

They were much older, and much wiser.

'It's a good idea, Mum. Thanks.'

'I know it's early days, but you want the child, don't you, Gertrude?'

'I'm frightened, Mum. I don't know about Charles. I mean, he's always away. But I will speak to the sisters.'

'Do that. And they'll be good to talk to. I'm sure.'

Louisa knew she was short of advice and floundered, she was just trying to deal with the wave of confusion Gertrude's news had brought.

'Speak to the sisters.'

'I will.'

Louisa sat in the old upright wooden chair and felt her head swim. Gertrude disappeared like a ghost from the flat.

Images flooded Louisa's troubled mind; the written message of some twenty years ago from her sister-in-law telling her that William had passed away while she was sitting in the same chair and nine months pregnant with Gertrude; the swarthy figure of Henry Benjamin moving in as a lodger and becoming more than that; then the trauma and the beatings and the alcohol; and despite Henry's letter last spring, for eight years a relative stability and serenity. She and the children had survived.

Now another ordeal had just appeared on the horizon.

Chapter 9

The summer sun had bleached the rose-patterned covers of the settee in the Lewis sisters' front room, but the current wan wintry sun would certainly not have the same effect. Gertrude looked around at the familiar interior of china, paintings, and the view over the fields to the wooded hill. Somehow life in this house had a feeling of calm and reason and the sisters brought serenity to their environment.

Lily Alice had told her to wait in the room while the sisters dealt with the arrival of new boarders from the nearby railway station.

Gertrude's anxiety deepened as she considered how her body had almost involuntarily been taken over by an unknown force. Sickness was just as much real as symbolic. She was no longer the person she had been just a few months ago. Her young mind ran rife with the thoughts of her newly found vulnerability, ill-repute and pain that had just loomed out of the mist and hit her before she had even planned her own future. How could she deal with a child with no father present on a permanent basis but, somehow, considering her own father who had died before she had even caught a glimpse of him and the drunken stepfather who had left them all cold and frightened, it may be that the status of a single mother offered more in the way of hope and welfare.

In short, her child would probably live through the same

incomplete family surroundings that she and her siblings had all experienced.

Would she really have wanted that for her children?

Familiar voices outside spoke of lodgings, keys and rooms. Approaching footsteps were heard on the gravel.

The Lewis sisters spoke to Lily Alice.

'You said Gertrude's indoors? It's her afternoon off.'

'She just said she would like to talk,' replied Lily Alice.

'I hope it's nothing serious,' said Anne Lewis.

Gertrude's mind swirled when the two ladies came into the room.

Starched and prim, but benevolent in their demeanour, they bore reason and goodwill with them. Only two years separated them, and many took them for twins. They had lived in the house all their lives and now let rooms for boarders, notably visiting clergy whose peaceful contact seemed to rub off on them.

'Hello Gertrude. What brings you here? You seem distressed.'

Marie looked on inquisitively.

'I came to ask you if you could help me, please.'

'How?' Anne asked.

'I don't know. That's the problem.'

She stuttered and looked away and then stared out at them from her mop of curly brown hair and glistening eyes knowing that in all circumstances they would understand her. For a moment she was lost for words. She couldn't implore; she could just offer desolation.

Marie held out her hand and led her to the settee.

'You can tell us, Gertrude.'

'I saw Mum today and she said it would be good to

speak to you, too.' She paused. 'I don't know how to say this but . . . I think I am expecting a child.'

The sisters looked at each other anxiously.

'Think, Gertrude?'

'I am fairly sure. I'm getting morning sickness and . . .'

She looked into the distance and wondered how she had said it.

'Well, just tell us who it is, Gertrude. Tell us.'

'It's Charlie's baby. But I don't know if he's even going to be here. It was as if we just fell in love and out of love every time we met. You know, one day he's here, the next he's gone, and he sends cards. How on earth am I going to deal with this? I know it's my fault and I should have thought, but we've known each other for three years. I thought it was safe.'

Gertrude wondered at the torrent of words describing the hopeless circumstances that she had found herself in.

The Lewis sisters looked at each other. A period of silence etched itself into the little group. An onlooker could easily have been mistaken in thinking that the scene was a sitting for a painter.

'Well, it's happened, Gertrude, and you must think carefully about what you, and your young man want.' said Annie, bringing them all back to reality.

'Can you write to him?' asked Marie.

'He's in Dublin. I'll send him a letter.'

'You're still very young Gertrude. You need help. If we can help, we will. Try to find out what Charles wants, and then we will see what can be done,' said Annie.

'Thank you.'

She raised her slim frame and moved towards the door.

The sisters escorted Gertrude to the large front door, and she trod the gravel path back to her room in the boarding house next door.

Once inside she felt the wave of distress hit her again. Nevertheless, she had spoken.

Speaking had transformed the muted pain into tomorrow's resolve and given her a veiled form of hope. She longed to speak to Charlie, too. But she couldn't, and what was he going to do or say in reply?

Now it would take several letters in her attempt to navigate the next steps of her life, or their lives. How precarious could that become with an itinerant soldier and an unexpected child on the way? It seemed no more than half of a step at a time.

She took out a sheet of paper and started to write.

Dear Charlie,

I hope all is well with you in Dublin.

I'm sorry to have to write this, but when we were together last in October we actually did more than we intended, because I am now expecting . . . if things go well, the baby will be born in June. What do you think we should do, Charlie? It's your child, too. We never meant to have a baby, did we? I know it's an accident.

I am worried and want you to help me if you can. When is your next furlough? Can you get leave? Please write back.

Lovingly,
Gertie.

Was I supposed to be a mother at twenty? she thought.

She sealed the letter and took it to the letter box at the end of the lane. Feelings of remorse and fear gnawed at her belly.

This walk to the letter box should not be for this.

As she was coming back to the house, the front door opened, and the figure of a young vicar emerged. He nodded at her and made his way to one of the churches in town.

The idea of confession ran through Gertrude's mind, but she was Church of England.

How she wished that the letter might bring her constructive and loving news from Dublin, but she could already envisage the shock on Charles' face as he opened it. He would be lost, too.

Dublin

Chapter 10

Charles's regiment had recently landed in Dublin and was currently garrisoned in the Portobello Barracks. Ireland was little different to what Charles had expected. The buildings, the tramcars, and horse-drawn carriages all reminded him of Portsmouth. But the greyness seemed to dominate for long periods, unlike the changeable skies over the Solent. The soldiers were given instructions to turn out and parade the next day.

The immense parade ground with its surrounding barracks was alive with the band's marching music; brass instruments, and the strident rapping of the drums. Private Charles Soloman had played his role as drummer boy for many years. He knew his part and the others knew he was proficient and reliable. They called him 'Sammy.' He handled sports well and bore a willowy light frame.

As they came to a halt for their inspection, Charles saw the bag of post being carried into the army's post office.

They were dismissed and he found a few cards and a letter. He took them back to his barracks and opened the letter from Gertrude.

Dear Charlie,

I hope all is well with you in Dublin.

I'm sorry to have to write this, but when we were together last in October we actually did more than we intended, because I am now expecting . . . if things go well, the baby will be born in June. What do you think we should do Charlie?

He read and reread that second line.

I'm sorry to have to write this, but when we were together last in October we actually did more than we intended, because I am now expecting . . .

Gradually the words sank in.

Charles stared up out of the high upper windows into the grey cold and overcast sky of Dublin and wished he had never opened the letter. Gertie, like him, had fallen into a situation that was all too common, yet easily avoided. His older and confident nature and her naïve youthfulness meant they had followed millions into the beckoning drama of illegitimacy.

'Yes, I am fond of her,' he thought aloud. 'She has been so much fun and happiness over the last two years . . . but expecting . . . whatever next, holy Jesus?'

'Has she really been so much fun?' said Private Glass, standing opposite.

'Eh, sorry, I just . . . I'm in a bit of trouble here.'

Glass came nearer.

'So, your sweetheart's in the family way?'

He leaned in on Charles wearing an ironic grin, and Charles cringed. Glass had a mighty frame.

'So, what are you gonna do about it, Sammy? Are you gonna stay with her or leave her?'

'I wish I knew.'

Glass picked up his kitbag and left, casting a glance over his shoulder at Charles who went through the motions of dealing with the shock. How, when, and why? What would he tell his parents? What would be the reaction of Gertrude's family? They had struck up a certain familiarity with him over the last three years.

Over and again he recalled the moments they had spent together and tried to fix times and places to meet. The last two years in Bordean camp had thrown him and Gertrude together. He had written local postcards to her wishing her family well and had also used the Lewis sisters at the boarding house as the conduit for his correspondence. Something greater than a casual relationship had grown out of their times together, and now this news had come too early, news so fresh and unnecessary, news that their last time together had brought an altogether different complexion to their lives, one that would now be permanent. It was an occurrence that would cast an enduring and terrible shadow over his period in Ireland, where he was supposed get on and build the next stage in his military career. He didn't like the fact that the past was dragging him back.

His error had opened up a new awkward path to negotiate which led away from the one he had already embarked on. He contemplated asking for leave, getting married, and spending the rest of his years as a soldier husband. He was twenty-seven and it was probably the logical thing to do. Gertrude was merely twenty and while he had on some occasions used her as a plaything, she had also played along. She had wanted a man, and he had given her that man. But what at first had seemed a light-hearted relationship had become a nightmare.

He recalled how the Lewis sisters had watched over her and tried to limit her evening escapades when the soldiers first came to town, but unbridled feverishness had pushed her out to meet him. He remembered that even her sister, Mabel, had encouraged her and seemed to expect the same in return from Gertrude. Mabel's postcards said as much, and her encrypted messages hid the text, but revealed the mischief that she borrowed from her older sister.

But no-one had anticipated this turn of events.

In short, fun and games had taken over and ratcheted up the price that would eventually be rung up on the till and Charlie had been caught up in it.

What's the cost for me? The end of the army as a roving soldier and a fairly organised yet disciplined life. It would mean the end of good sports, music, and friends, the end of seeing other places. I'd have to start trying to fit into civilian life when all my life has been built around the army.

The door opened again and the battalion with their chatter, laughter, and bustling behaviour invaded the large room. An officer came in with them. The men turned around when he called them to attention. Charles saw the silhouette of Sergeant Erin and stood up.

'Gentlemen!'

'Yes, Sergeant!'

'A good number of you will be part of the football team for Friday. So, there won't be any leave this weekend and we'll be on manoeuvres next week. You'll be away for several days.'

Charles looked across at Erin and realized that he was being moved further away from the context he needed to be in. External forces had spun him out of Gertrude's reach into another place and time and, however well intended he may have been, his grasp on events and his desire to grasp events was receding with the orders being handed out to the men right now. He closed his eyes.

* * *

Two days later in the wintry cold and damp the soldiers emerged from the barracks and fell in. Private Glass caught up with Charles again.

'So, Sammy, have you made up your mind?'

'About what?' he replied, pretending he didn't know.

'Don't try that with me, Sammy. Most of the battalion will soon find out that your young lady is expecting. You're not the first, nor the last. It is the lot of a good many soldiers. They have the courage to go to war, but can't handle family, women, and wives.'

'How do you expect the battalion will find out?'

'News travels fast and rumours come out of nothing sometimes,' warned Glass.

Charles thought he could still bluff his way through.

'Are you going to take it up with the sergeant?'

Charles remained silent.

They passed the outer gates of the barracks where the bare elm trees stood and dripped, the railings glinted with water, and the roads with puddles. They turned into the road leading to the sports fields.

'See this, Sammy?'

The men marched past the church.

'See what it's called?' murmured Glass. 'It says, 'The Church of Mary Immaculate Refuge of Sinners'. See, you don't have to go far. It's two minutes from Portobello.'

'Drop it, will you?' Charles replied.

He looked up again at the lettering above the four sober columns to the church and wondered if the building was a law court or a church. Images of Gertrude began to crowd his mind. He recalled her slight form, her wiry brown hair, her high forehead, her oval face and those appealing, inquiring, trustful eyes. She was rather the smaller version of his tall supple frame and it struck him that perhaps their physical likenesses had brought them together? He recalled her on the same old chair in her room, in her long skirt and thin white turtle-neck pullover adorned with his locket. Her gentleness and his frame. And now they would drift apart, locked into the same gnawing sense of desperation. For one it meant *responsibility* and for the other, *escape.*

Maydurham

Chapter 11

William Lyndsey often spoke to Ada about his return from France, but always kept it to a simple account.

One evening they had cleared the pub and were clambering up to their rooms when a detail in the painting hanging in the stairway caught William's eye. It was a picture of the town square, and in one corner there was a horse and gig led by a farmer. It was a fairly rural scene, nothing of particular interest, but William felt drawn to it.

As he stared, he tried to tell Ada that it reminded him of the day he stepped off the train in Devon when he was twelve, but he knew she had already anticipated what he was going to say, only to dismiss it as 'times gone by', or memories that one can re-invoke but not put flesh on.

For William, what he saw was not so much a memory but a symptom of something that had cast doubts on his rightful place in this world. That much, he would not say, nor expound on, yet that much he would feel in his bones.

Belonging somewhere is a strong sentiment but when it is tampered with, diluted or confused, the human copes, but just coping should not be man's destiny, he thought.

* * *

He remembered his last moments in Cannes at the age of eleven when they put him into the *chaise,* his trunk behind. He embraced his mother, Eliza, his father, William, and his brothers and sisters. Looking up he captured the mountainous ridge, the pine trees, their dark-green slopes and their decoratively constructed villas running down to the blue. Outside his parents' quarters, he heard the rustle of plants and greenery and the spades splitting the dry earth as the gardeners continued their work in *Château Thorenc* where they now lived. Just a stone's throw from *Le Chateau Sainte Anne.*

The driver turned the horse round and exited the grounds. Accompanied by other travellers, William surveyed the scene as they descended the dusty road, running through the elegant architecture of the villas and *châteaux* to the railway station where they would meet the steam train from Nice. He enjoyed the snatches of conversation of passers-by, the wafting breezes and the gentle climate of the Mediterranean for the last time.

* * *

One thousand miles away, the rolling downs and wooded hills of Devon separated and scattered its population into rural hamlets and virtually inaccessible dwelling places through the necessity of producing crops and animal breeding which brought value and yield to the land. Squires ran the countryside and watched after the livelihood of the population, generally with a degree of benevolence and sympathy. In particular, they were kind to those people who helped in the gardens of the manor, managed the farmsteads, or the local watermills belonging to the family. Thus, human ties and dependencies were built fashioning a close-knitted community based on mutual interest.

The Squire also helped build schools, develop adult education, improve horticulture, and encouraged inhabitants, through the building of cottages, to dwell in the villages to maintain the local economy and their own livelihoods. In this area the Squire was a Liberal and brought new ideas to bear on tradition. Already immensely rich, he gained further wealth by marrying into and accumulating a further estate. He was, nevertheless, conscious of fulfilling his responsibilities for the welfare of the community,

The estate where William Lyndsey's father had worked before moving to France looked out over the villages near Exeter. The hills rolled proudly from east to west, enabling their inhabitants to watch the sun climb to its zenith before plunging. They also surveyed the green meadows where the river followed its course and often overflowed into the pastures of the grazing livestock. The road was forded at many a place and travellers enjoyed the view from the safety of their carriage or from the recently built railway line running beside it. The river was tidal, so nature breathed in and out with watery lungs every minute of the day.

The horse and trap were waiting as a few people left the station. Young William emerged and looked around at the unfamiliar surroundings: a white-washed Victorian station building, a yard, and a bridge. He noticed the plain and saw a river had flooded the road alongside the railway line. The damp here contrasted vividly with the heat and unfettered sun of the Mediterranean. The mud darkened the grassy roadside and the trees still dripped with the morning's rain; sights William had rarely had to cast his eyes upon.

At just eleven years old he was sensitive to the disparities in culture and environment and struck by the darker colours couched in the unfamiliar silence of a remote and hushed rural backwater. It was austere.

His grandfather had brought the trap down to collect him, a grandfather he had never known or seen. The farmer.

'You must be William Halden junior. Pleased to see you, Will,' a voice called.

'Thanks. You must be Grandad.'

They hoisted his trunk onto the back of the trap.

'We know each other from letters and cards, but it's nice to see you in real life. All the way from France! That's some journey. Sorry that we couldn't organize the weather for you.'

He turned the trap around, and they worked the narrow lanes and hills until they arrived way above the meadows. The rising lanes and ditches were often sheltered or overgrown by the trees and bushes on the banks, and neither of them had a view of the fields below. The horse knew its way. The final narrow mud track led up to the farmhouse and the barns.

Grandfather John Halden's family was large, and William had already found it a challenge to navigate the maelstrom of relationships, births, and deaths that his father had related to him. Nevertheless, the only other family fixture at the farm seemed to be his young uncle. The others had left. Robert occupied part of the farmhouse and welcomed his nephew as he alighted from the trap. Robert was nine years younger than his brother, and his youthful, healthy figure caught William's attention, almost as if he was viewing his father at a younger age.

'You look like Dad, but a bit younger,' William said.

'Really? Well, my French nephew, *bonjour, comment ça va?*'

'Bien, merci,' William replied.

'You must tell us all about Cannes and my brother's life there.'

The farmhouse stood to the left of the farm entrance and its main yard, and the two men hauled William's trunk in. Their retriever harried them and wagged his tail.

So, this is where I must live now.

Farm work and a rural existence seemed to stretch out before him, but he hadn't been prepared for this degree of rurality and desolate remoteness. The sunny walk down to the sea had gone. The views of the luxuriant gardens and stately houses had been whisked away.

His grandmother, Anne, cajoled him saying that this was a change for a continental gentleman, but didn't realise the poignancy of her remark.

Having carried his trunk upstairs, his relatives opened a door.

Looking around the low-windowed bedroom, furnished sparingly, he noticed a scholar's desk just beneath a window overlooking the green slope down to the edge of the field, a painting of an ancestor over the small bed and bedside table, and a large wardrobe opposite the window seeming likely to topple at any moment because of the uneven wooden floor.

Having surveyed the room, William concluded there had been an overwhelming change in his life.

* * *

'Are you coming up?' Ada shouted.

'On my way,' William answered, although he felt lost to another world.

'Why can't I shake off these memories? Why can't I go back? Is life in Maydurham really that bad?

Chapter 12

Olive sat with Gertrude. She had come straight from her work at *'Cossington'* to see her because Louisa had told her of the predicament. Gertrude did not resent her sister's presence but seeing her made her wish for the one person she really needed and who she worried was never going to show up. The letter had gone. His reply would take time.

'Why didn't you tell me more about him, Gert?'

'It's not that I didn't tell you about him. You knew we were courting, somehow.'

'No, it wasn't like that at all. We know that you met the soldiers with the other girls in town, we knew that Charlie was pleased to be with you whenever he was billeted nearby, but we didn't really suspect that it was that serious . . .'

'Well, I began to think it was and now I am expecting his child.'

'I know. Mother told me. And I am sure I don't know what to say, Gert. I wish I could help.'

'Maybe, you can. If you would just be frank and tell me your thoughts.'

'Well, it just strikes me that I don't see how we are really going to cope unless you and your soldier find a home and build a family. But from what it seems, that may never happen, which means mum and all of us will have to take care of the little one. So, I feel bound to say that as much as we all love children this *has come* as a surprise and none of us really knows the right course of action yet. And you are only just twenty. For the moment it's really up to you and your young man.'

Gertrude had the answer.

'I have just written to him. He doesn't know yet. He's in Ireland.'

'Hmm. Perhaps that's just as it would suit him.'

'Don't be like that, Olly.'

'Sorry. But, as they say, '*out of sight, out of mind*', you know.'

'Yes.'

Gertrude had been on the receiving end of precisely what she had asked for: her sister's frank straightforward thoughts.

Olive stood up. The brown wainscot panelling and cream-coloured paint above provided the background for the scene. The two women looked at each other, both slim and relatively tall. Gertrude with her rebellious curls and Olive with her wavy auburn hair tied in a neat bun. They held the moment in silence, wishing that the dusk would take their pain away. Then they descended the stairs.

Gertrude stood at the little back door and watched her sister disappear down the lane in the half-light.

As she turned back to her door, she heard footsteps on the gravel and saw Anne Lewis coming towards her.

'Gertrude, if you have a moment or two, we have thought about something.'

'Of course.'

The two women stood on the doorstep of Gertrude's dwelling. She contemplated the grey outlines of the snowdrops just beginning to bud in the border.

Then the spring flowers would soon be on their way and after them a new child. The plan of things seemed about half right in the natural course of events.

Anne Lewis hesitated and then spoke.

'Gertrude, we know this will be a tormenting time for you.'

She paused and sighed, looked at Gertrude.

Merely a young girl with trusting eyes, Miss Lewis thought.

'Marie and I have put our minds together and maybe we have part of an answer to the more vexatious part of your predicament. If ever, it is not yours and Charles' intention to have this child, then we know of a place near London where you may have the child and decide your own destinies. They are good people and they understand the terrible circumstances of women today.'

Gertrude looked even more lost.

Anne Lewis paused again and then pursued in a gentle tone.

'Life for a mother can be wretched. Especially when she is pregnant with no man in the vicinity. You know this. We all know this, and I don't have to paint a more forlorn picture: she has much to do not to shrink from the looks of others that single her out as an odd woman. And it happens to women from all and every rank.'

'Marie and I have never found husbands, so we were looked upon as incapable of marriage and family life, and people were keen to gossip. We all know words just heap wretchedness on the ordeal itself. But today we are older and have our boarding house to run, as you know, so people's focus turned from us some time ago. Maybe, if you should ever find yourself in the same position, we could help to protect you too. At least until such time as those particular onlookers have moved on to other objects of speculation.'

'You are young, so mean-spirited or vicious people who want to turn your life upside down will talk. Reputations are won in a moment and stick for years. Only close friends and family can really help to protect.'

'In the last twenty or so years new braver women have been emerging and are helping to banish some of the awful ideas and stereotypes of women that we are supposed to embody. Of course, it will take a long time for people to accept those who don't fit the mould, and their gossip will find its victims. Certainly '*the fallen woman*' is probably the most hideous form of insult cast at the misfortunate by those hiding behind their biblical morals instead of taking aim at the real culprit, the heathen male, who has comparatively little to fear . . . I am sure you will agree.'

Gertrude did not really follow the words. She had the impression of listening to a sermon. Her immediate worries were about Charlie's reply, which may never come. She understood the gist of what Miss Lewis was saying, but her mind couldn't pin down reason and argument. Miss Lewis had said something about torment and protection and that had resonated. Other things Miss Lewis said seemed to strike a moral tone. Nevertheless, Gertrude knew she was standing on her doorstep with somebody trying to reach out to her, but for the moment she was still overwhelmed by the realization of her irreversible and helpless predicament.

'Gertrude, I know that what I have said is difficult to feel or understand at this moment but let's talk again . . .

whenever you like. And whatever happens you will keep your job here.'

'Thank you, Miss Lewis.'

Tears rolled down her cheeks. Her chin hung down, her curls fell, and she pulled a small, embroidered handkerchief from the sleeve of her thin woollen jersey.

'Where are you, Charlie?' she muttered to herself.

Miss Lewis crossed the yard to her front door.

Night had finally settled upon the house.

PART 3

The Haven of Hope – That which *once* was Mine

Claydon

Chapter 13

Burdened by her suitcase and feeling the weight of her belly, Gertrude stood and recovered her breath after mounting the steps from the station.

The high street was very different. It was broad and stretched out into the hazy distance. The buildings here were taller and more fashionable than those in Maydurham. Brass globe lanterns hanging from their ornate mountings caught Gertrude's eye. They decorated the pavement before the *Fox and Hounds*, whose frontage was decorated with mullioned bow windows and a high overhanging pointed gable.

The tramcar stopped just before the public house and took on two men dressed for business. Barrow boys parked their wares at the kerb. At the hospital entrance a young girl sold flowers from her parked pony and trap. Her long dress and hat reminded Gertrude of flower sellers she had seen in Portsmouth, and the times she had brought home bunches for her mother.

Spring was upon the town and some of the shops had already lowered their awnings but not to keep off the rain. The sun blanched the ladies' prim blouses and cast shadows over the foreheads of the capped and hatted pedestrians.

The grating and clanking of the tramcar wheels in their

lines, the shouts from each side of the broad thoroughfare, the bustle of the horses and carts manoeuvering past each other to avoid the oncoming tram sounded so foreign to the short and parochial High Street that had been the backdrop of her life until then.

She stopped beside the flower girl and looked in at the hospital grounds and contemplated taking a tramcar to her destination but reconsidered when a passer-by looked at her form and told her it was probably no more than fifteen minutes on foot. Walking had not yet become an awkward or painful exercise.

Another tramcar clanked by. The people on the open top deck could have been on a sightseeing tour.

Pedestrians and shopkeepers, urchins and girls like her filled the scene, and Gertrude wondered if they had the same unrelenting worries as her.

Her life had changed in so many ways and without warning: from spinster to future single mother and all that accompanied her new status. The child's and her own future stood at a fork in the road. Were they one and the same, or were they to be divided and lost to each other forever after?

The flower girl reminded her of the day she had brought home a bunch of flowers for her mother.

* * *

The gesture came after the dreadful moments she had suffered on the end of one of her mother's tirades condemning her wantonness with the soldiers coming and going in the town centre. That was more than a year ago. Her mother had been right. Gertrude hadn't seen what was wrong but wanted to make up for the hurt she was causing.

'Mother, I brought you these. I'm sorry.'

Louisa had just come home. She looked at her daughter. Taking off her hat and readying herself to start the evening she wondered what Gertrude was trying to tell her.

'What is this, Gertrude?'

'I am just trying to say sorry.'

'Do you want my blessing?'

'No, that's not it.'

'You know very well what I think and what others think about you running around with the servicemen that come into this town.'

'I don't run around with them. There's only really one I like, but he's always with a group, so I end up being part of his group.'

'The family has enough worries trying to keep itself together, what with your stepfather and his shame cast upon us all. I don't want and I don't need anymore.'

'I know.'

'Well don't get involved with these people, then. They're wasting your time.'

Gertrude swallowed.

'I'm sorry if I should give you cause to fear, but my being here is mere fortune, too.'

'What do you mean?'

'Well, if dad had died six months earlier, I wouldn't be here. Perhaps I needed a father. Maybe I still need one.'

'Look Gertrude, what is done is done and I don't see

what fortune has to do with you meddling with soldiers.'

'I suppose, I might as well keep the flowers.'

'If you so wish. It was a kind gesture Gertrude, but I'll only give you my blessing when you have sorted your head out. Rules are set down to guide the thoughts of those who stray.'

Gertrude sighed at the moral turn of their conversation, turned and trudged down the stairs, the flowers in her hand.

'I'll give them to Miss Annie,' she said to herself.

Moments like this had caused her great dismay and seemed to point to a rocky path ahead.

* * *

Following the pavement in her daydream she reached the park and pond and then crossed to the other side of the road having been drawn by the sight of a rather majestically columned building with broad white steps leading up to the front. Its life seemed to be captured and held in the frame of the garden as if immovable and permanent. Straight lines and symmetry abounded. The grounds were manicured.

Holding her suitcase in one hand and the iron railings in the other, Gertrude felt the chaos within her.

How had she found herself here? Miles from home, bearing a letter of introduction to persons she had never set eyes on and three months from bearing a child she had never intended.

In her moments of quiet before embarking on her journey, she had sat at home and felt the moves and little kicks and known the body within her: the life and breath of the soul that was partly hers. She had rubbed her belly and communed with the being; spoken, hummed and listened for the sound of a child. *Her child.*

She crossed the road again and saw a sign marked '*Haven of Hope. A Christian Mission.*', opened the garden gate, mounted the steps and knocked on the door of an imposing new house with three Moorish arches and three storeys. Next to it loomed the *Congregation Church* tower. A young lady beckoned her in. Gertrude's appearance required no questions. Another tramcar clattered by as the door shut behind her.

Chapter 14

The young girl showed Gertrude up the broad staircase, which looked out over the church. Her bedroom had a view of the generously large gardens running along the backs of the imposing houses built over the last twenty years. The view from the front of her new address gave on to the fine mansion called 'The Cedars', whose railings Gertrude had clung to. In the days to come she would occasionally go and stand and wonder at the remarkable white building with its fine front gable, upper-windows and white pilaster Doric columns at its entrance below.

Much of it seemed unreal and beyond the world she had just left behind: her room overlooking the fields and the neighboring hangers. And even more unreal when she thought about the family's flat over the shop in Dog Alley where the police had picked up her stepfather.

A woman dressed in a nurse's uniform appeared at the top of the stairs and asked her if she had travelled far and then helped her settle into her room.

'Later this afternoon, I will take you to see Miss Hurd and she will explain how the Mission works. We'll take the tram. It's quite a distance from here and this house is temporary. The main office is in South Claydon.'

Gertrude looked at the nurse and thought that her life had just become an anonymous medical condition in an unknown metropolis; something she had not anticipated nor hoped for at the age of twenty. The Lewis sisters had sworn to help her. She so wished they hadn't had to, but the dreadful motion of time and human error had taken things out of her grasp. She felt dejected and lost.

* * *

The tram dropped them, and they proceeded to the house in Hirst Road. A slim woman with wavy brown hair and angular features opened the door and welcomed them.

'Thank you, Laura, for bringing Miss Kimble to us.'

'She arrived this morning,' the nurse replied. 'Gertrude, this is Miss Hurd.'

The hallway formed a hexagon of closed doors to Gertrude. She removed her hat. A pile of books and several copies of *Votes for Women* sat on a low table near one of the doors.

'If you would like to come with me,' said Miss Hurd.

Gertrude followed her into a darkened study with two desks and a marble fireplace. A large wooden clock, a barometer, and an empty vase made up the occupants of the mantelpiece. She noticed several bibles and a little proverb pinned to the wall: '*It is love that keeps the world warm.*'

Miss Hurd offered her a seat.

'I am afraid Mrs. Willis is out at the moment, but I am sure you will see her shortly. Let me tell you a little about the Haven. Or, perhaps, you already know a little.'

'Well, not much. I must say I am rather lost.'

'Well, where you are staying at the moment, the London Road building, is temporary until we find other permanent premises for the Mission. I think it's a lovely house and I am sure you will find yourself comfortable there. Laura is a good nurse. She takes good care and will give you plenty of help. Your baby is due in June, if I am not mistaken.'

'Yes, that's right,' Gertrude replied. 'What do I do until then?'

'You will help Laura and other nurses who take care of the deliveries of babies and the welfare of the other mothers. You will help with the cooking and cleaning and also the gardening there. That way you will be able to make yourself useful and feel part of the Mission and understand its routines and even its aspirations.'

'Do you know if you would like to have your baby adopted?' Miss Hurd continued.

Gertrude looked out the window and let her thoughts stray into the spring greenery of bushes and trees.

'Well, perhaps, we can talk about that a little later.' concluded Miss Hurd. 'Have you had any contact with the father recently?'

A tear slid down Gertrude's face and she took a handkerchief from the sleeve of her cardigan.

'I am sorry, Gertrude. This is an all-too-common situation, and you should not blame yourself or anybody. Today's society is unforgiving and spiteful and that is largely why Miss Willis has devoted herself to reversing the tide of injustice that women suffer today. Men run their lives as they wish and we women seem to be the last of their thoughts, but the first of their desires!'

Gertrude saw a brief reflection in the window and a few seconds later a grey-haired lady appeared in the room.

'Hello, you must be Miss Kimble?' she said, and Miss Hurd introduced Mrs. Janet Willis.

She was tall and of stocky build and twenty years older than Miss Hurd. Her grey hair was parted in the middle and tied back in a bun.

'Pleased to meet you, Mrs. Willis. I've heard a little about you and the Mission from Miss Hurd here and the Lewis sisters who employ me at the boarding house.'

'Welcome, Gertrude. Although these are exceptional times, I am nevertheless pleased to shake your hand and tell you we will look after you. The Mission will provide you with hope and comfort,' she started. 'May I ask you a question, though?'

'Of course,' replied Gertrude.

'Gertrude, who knows you are here?'

'Well, just my older sister, Olive, and Mum. That's all in the family. The others have been told I am working for acquaintances of Miss Lewis for a short time up here. Anyway, it's best if my other brothers and sisters don't learn about it yet.'

'So, you have quite a family? You are lucky. Of course, discretion is our motto. You may rest assured. We shall always keep your secret.'

Gertrude felt the baby kick in her womb and she altered her position.

'You know, Mrs. Willis, I really hoped I could take the baby home . . . but then the town would all know, and I don't know if I could keep my job with Miss Marie and Miss Annie, and they have already helped so much in getting me here.'

'We still have time to talk this over,' said Mrs. Willis. 'Once you have spent some time with the other girls, maybe you'll be able to form a better judgement. I believe the Lewis's also paid for a part of your welfare here.'

'Yes, they did. I am quite indebted to them.'

'God works in mysterious ways, you know. And faith is part of our mission here as well. So many lost children and mothers need the help of the Lord. I do hope you will benefit from our daily Bible classes.'

'Yes, I hope so,' said Gertrude wonderingly.

'You know, Gertrude, you, like many others, have come to us at your wit's end, floundering. Most are sick with black despair and some even go as far as to think of suicide. And the word that greets you here is 'hope'. 'Hope' despite the world being against you. 'Hope' despite being deceived and deserted. 'Hope' is our mission and 'love' is our means of restoring lives that have been shattered.'

Gertrude listened to the Christian message and felt that Mrs. Willis had understood the anguish that she had carried for so many months.

'I am sure that you will find your feet here and later when you have decided, we'll talk about the arrangements after the birth . . .whether you would like the child to stay here, be adopted or placed in foster care. As you know, if you agree to adoption, then things are completely out of your hands.'

The words 'adoption' and 'foster care' felt alien. The baby was hers. It kicked in her womb. She still couldn't understand how two short journeys by train and one by tramcar had brought her here to this Haven managed by this remarkable lady who helped so many young single mothers. Then through the window she caught sight of the wind in the bushes and trees and compared the view with that from her own bedroom window.

Suddenly the life of a baby and the sadness of her soul

converged into an abhorrent feeling of misplaced time and space.

Miss Hurd reminded Gertrude she had a number of weeks of housework and cooking ahead of her before and after the birth of her child. It was part of the arrangement.

The next thing she knew was that Mrs. Willis was on her feet and gently helping her to hers.

'My life is all askew,' she wanted to say, but 'goodbye and thank you' fell from her lips as if in a nightmare. Mrs. Willis only smiled enigmatically, nodded and remained silent. Miss Hurd helped her to the door where Laura was waiting to conduct Gertrude back to her new imposing abode.

The newspaper *Votes for Women* caught her eye again and Laura noticed Gertrude's interest.

'You have heard about the Suffragettes, haven't you?'

'Yes.'

'Well, it's their newspaper.'

'I wasn't sure. Thank you.' Gertrude replied. 'They're very brave.'

* * *

Gertrude climbed the stairs again and reached her landing. Another pregnant girl seemingly of the same age stood at her bedroom door.

'Hello, I am Daisy. I heard you are Gertrude. Are you coming to the Bible class tomorrow?'

Broadmere

Chapter 15

Rose was younger. She was a Harding. Barely two years separated her from Gertrude and whereas her step-sister bore the more angular visage of her father, Rose bore the more rounded face of her mother. Both were close to each other and they had a similar feature: their curls were nearly the same, but Rose tied her hair back. When they were children, wherever Gertrude went, Rose could often be found tagging along. Gertrude wore a challenging or critical look where Rose wore one of naivety and instant belief. Gertrude was spontaneous whereas Rose wished she knew how to be.

Louisa had cultivated a close family, and the complicity of the sisters heartened her until Gertrude became involved with her soldier friend. Rose seemed to slip into her own world after that or attach herself to Fred whenever he had a book to share.

As she grew older, Rose's mouth became a half moon and her eyes turned even rounder with her circular steel-rimmed glasses, which pinched her nose. She lacked the delicacy of Gertrude and lived in the hope of finding someone. Sadly, unlike her siblings, she was destined to spinsterhood. Even in her teens she sensed that she could not please the young men Gertrude and her friends met, and hung back from the groups that assembled in the summer evenings in the square. Though Rose looked at them, few turned to look back at her.

Then came the time for work and the usual call of domestic service, and Rose proved to be the traveller in the family, moving between Maydurham, the Isle of Wight and the fringes of Guildford where she now found herself.

She had been told that Gertrude had 'gone away to work in Claydon' and felt her absence, as well as the workload she endured at Hazel Dene in Broadmere. The occupant, Mrs. Tyndale, ran the large house dedicated to arts and crafts while her husband travelled the world painting for travel books. Rose sometimes sat and admired his paintings when her body ached too much. The images enabled her to escape. She travelled to Egypt through them, inspecting the streets of Cairo, the mosques, the tall minarets, feeling the heat and the dust, almost smelling the donkeys and their burdens.

Some days she felt exhausted, even feverish, and her limbs ached. She couldn't understand these terrible moments. She was hardly a mature woman. Why should she suffer so much? One day, however, she noticed blotches on her cheeks. Mrs. Tyndale saw her seated in the front room and entered.

'Rose?'

'Sorry, Mrs. Tyndale, I had a terrible feeling of weariness that overcame me. I will be all right in a few moments.'

'Rose, you don't look at all well.'

Rose's bun held back her flowing curls and her look of sincerity caught Mrs. Tyndale. Her employee was too young to complain of weariness, and she knew there was truth in everything Rose said. On closer examination, she saw Rose was red and feverish.

Rose stood up, patted down her apron, and moved towards the fireplace where she had been working.

'Rose, you know, I have a very good doctor friend who may be able to help you.'

Rose sighed. She didn't really know what to say, having attributed the febrile moments and pains to her menstrual cycle. Then again, the blotches on her face were giving her cause for concern.

'Thank you, Mrs. Tyndale. If it is not too much bother for you, I would willingly accept.'

'Of course. I will speak to him and we'll make an appointment for you. You're not even twenty. We ought not to overlook something.'

Rose turned, caught sight of her image in the mirror above the mantelpiece, and collapsed.

* * *

When she came around, she saw the ceiling of her room, the outline of the window, the view down the garden, and two pairs of eyes staring at her. The man's face was not familiar, but she turned her head and recognized Mrs. Tyndale.

She raised herself from her bed and fell back. The pain in her limbs and her fever caught her.

'I am afraid she will not be back on her feet until her temperature goes down,' the doctor said.

Mrs. Tyndale turned to Rose.

'Don't worry,' she told her. 'You must rest as long as it takes for you to get better.'

Rose looked at Mrs. Tyndale and lapsed back into the

comfort of the pillow. The returning pain and onset of delirium would take time to subside.

* * *

Rose watched from her bed as a tall swarthy man left the town square and ran through the Moorish archway into the house, scattering the hens and flapping pigeons. He looked out of the deep doorway and seemed to wait, then resolutely closed the old wooden feature. The sun poured down into the dusty quadrangle. She saw another man in long grey robes and a skullcap cross the square and the sound of braying came from the camel that had appeared just below the minaret. Rose tried to hold the stone column opposite the doorway to catch her breath, but the stone column disappeared and crumbled to the earth. Lying on her back, Rose saw the decorative mashrabiya balconies in the street. Gertrude pulled her up and held her hand until she had finally dragged Rose out of the sun into the darkened room where the two young women looked at each other in silence. In the corner next to the large open hearth sat a soldier that Rose seemed to recognise.

'Mother will be here soon,' said Gertrude. 'It's too hot here for me. I'm going to the back garden.'

Rose watched her go into the back yard where the small courthouse stood, and they pulled her father out of the cell; he looked doleful. Mother stood by and they couldn't speak. They could only touch his shirt sleeves as they led him away.

'We must go now,' said Louisa. 'I have work to do for Mrs. Warren.'

Rose turned to Fred and asked him if he had seen the butterflies on her face. She struggled to her feet but couldn't even stand long enough to look into her bedroom mirror.

'Show me, Fred,' Rose tried to say. Fred was silent. He hadn't heard her effort to speak. He had picked up a book and seemed lost.

'I can't breathe, Fred. I can't breathe, Fred.'

* * *

Mrs. Tyndale watched over Rose for a while as she tossed and turned and then quietly left the room.

Maydurham

Chapter 16

Louisa and Olive sat in the flat above the shop. Below, the bell rang, and customers came and went. Mr. Rowswell served and chatted. It was early evening and spring had finally put leaves on the sycamore in the churchyard and the Avenue was beginning to hide itself under its new green cloak. Gertrude had been gone a month and the two elders, mother and daughter, reflected on the decision to send Gertrude away. They had decided that it was better to see Gertrude far from the townsfolk's curious glances and subsequent idle gossip. The Lewis sisters had helped immensely, both financially and through their knowledge of several homes for single mothers in the London suburbs.

In the family, still only Louisa and Olive knew Gertrude had gone away to give birth. The Lewis sisters had suggested that Gertrude's departure might be hidden behind the story of her being asked to do some temporary work in a boarding house belonging to acquaintances of the two sisters.

Despite the facade there was always the risk that somebody would surmise or stumble on the truth, but the two women knew they had been able to manage things thus far.

Louisa had moments of regret; Olive thought they could, perhaps, try to bring up the child themselves. Gertrude was a fairly popular person about town. The family had preserved its reputation after Henry had been removed and the matriarchy had set the wheels for survival in motion. How much would the arrival of a child to an unmarried mother affect them?

Quite naturally, all of the sisters hoped for the man who would await them at the altar and provide a happy family, safe from the realm of drunkenness, violence and illegitimate chidren.

None had found that man.

Gertrude in her effervescence had struck out first but had fallen foul of circumstances.

'The babe will be there in June,' said Olive.

'Poor little thing. I never thought we'd find ourselves in a situation like this,' Louisa sighed.

'If only we could have them both back here,' mused Olive.

'Then Gertrude has to give up work to look after the baby. Rose is away, too, and Mabel is just beginning to make a living in dressmaking. That means a nanny and we can't afford that,' Louisa replied and continued:

'According to Miss Annie, the baby can be brought up at the Mission and later placed with a foster family, and, as it grows up, it won't perhaps need to know who the parents were or are. She said some wealthy families, too, are keen to adopt kids, because they can't have them. It's not as if the baby is likely to be abandoned or maltreated. Maybe the child will end up happy and loved as much as Gertie could have done for it. I am sure I don't know the answer to this one . . . If I ever see that soldier of hers, I will skin him alive.'

'Gertrude still seems to be fond of him, judging from her letters. But she also seems to be coming around to the reality of her own mistake and his total lack of responsibility,' Olive said.

Deep down the two women knew they would err on the side of caution and discretion, if ever it was necessary to advise Gertrude. Obviously, the future of Gertrude's baby did not lie directly in their hands.

'Gertrude has a mind of her own, you know,' said Louisa.

Olive heard the postman downstairs and collected the mail.

She found a postcard from Broadmere from Rose.

Dear Mum and family,

Have been rather poorly but getting better Mrs. Tyndale has asked for me to see a doctor I haven't been able to work for two days I hope to be in town on S.

Love from Rose.

Louisa seemed worried. Olive watched her features.

'There's something not quite right there,' said Louisa. 'She has moments when she's obviously poorly and for no reason.'

'What shall we write back?'

'We'll have to ask her if she wants to see Dr. Bradbury here, or if Mrs. Tyndale wants her to see somebody in Broadmere.'

Olive fetched a card from the shop below and wrote her short message. The girls all wrote; mother did, too, but tended not to. When she had put her pen down and added a stamp, she turned to Louisa.

'Mother,' she said tentatively. 'I think I've met a man and I thought that . . .'

Olive paused.

'What do you mean, 'think you've met a man', Olive?' Louisa asked with a worried air, fearing the worst.

'Well, you know a few years ago when I was at grandad's before he died, one of his neighbours came in. He's in the navy and we started talking . . . and I think he's nice. He's handsome and has a rather fine moustache. He's from a rather big family. There are eight of them. He said he's in the marines.'

'So you think you've met him?' said a much-relieved and almost humorous Louisa.

'Yes, well, yes, I've met a man,' replied Olive a little flustered, discovering her mother's tone and seeing the glint in her eye. ' I met him again a few months ago by accident on the platform at the station and we travelled down to Pompey together. Then a few weeks ago he invited me for a drink.'

'So, what's his name?'

'Tom. Tom Hill. His family is still in the village. Grandma will know them. If you see her, you can ask.'

'Well, I'm pleased for you Ollie.'

'Thanks, Mum. I'll post the card and get back to the Avenue. Oh, and I have asked Mabel to come down to Southsea this Saturday. She said she'd like to. Maybe we'll see Lily.'

As she left the flat Olive noticed Rose's postcard album on the dresser near the fireplace; it was already full and certain cards poked out of the covers. Her young sister was a keen collector. It had now become a *sine qua non* that any journey by any member of the family or friends should include sending a card to Rose. Rose was popular and gentle, but the bouts of sickness had started to hinder the youthful liveliness of her body and mind. Rose would also be the first to help Gertie, whenever she was needed. As the elder, that relieved Olive to a certain degree.

Louisa, too, put on her bonnet, left the flat and headed for Mrs. Warren's.

Never a dull moment, she thought.

Chapter 17

Having unlocked their main entrance, Ada and William Lindsey stood on the threshold of their public house. The April weather was fine, and they shaded their eyes as the sun poured down over the church tower into their open doorway. The name of the licensee, William L. Halden, proudly printed in the upper part of the doorframe announced the bearded person who stood below adorning a smart dark-grey matching waistcoat and trousers, a modern cap and a long-sleeved white shirt. Ada was smaller and wore her large white apron over her emerald-coloured bustle dress. As much as she was ready to launch into her day's duties, so William seemed happy to take in the surroundings before busying himself.

'Reminds me of . . .' said William.

'Don't say it,' Ada interjected.

'Talking of travel, have you seen the Kimbles lately?' William asked.

'No, why?'

'I think Gertrude has moved out of Borough House.'

'Really?'

'Louisa told me she's gone up to a place near London to do some work for the Lewis's.'

'I never knew they had acquaintances up there.'

'She said she'd probably be up there for six months or so.'

Ada looked out at the square and a thought crossed her mind.

'That's what Louisa said?'

'Yes, why?'

'Does Gertrude's young man have people up there?'

'No, they're West Country or Sussex.'

'He hasn't been seen for some time, has he?' Ada said, reflectively.

'No, he's probably in Ireland now.'

'I suppose she'll be expecting him in the furlough season. I wonder what work she's doing.'

'Louisa said it was for another boarding house.'

They set about their cleaning work and William carried crates to the rear storeroom. Just as he was closing the door, he caught sight of Mabel rounding the corner on her way to her shop.

'Hello, Mabel, how are things going?'

Mabel cast her rather solemn but perspicacious and playful eyes on Mr. Halden.

'Hello, Mr. Halden. Thank you for asking. All's going very well at the draper's and I have plenty to do.'

'I hear Gertrude's left the Lewis's for a while.'

'Yes, she's working in Claydon.'

'Claydon? My parents spent time there, too. You, know, when they came back from France, they were there for a few years. It's a small world.'

Mabel hoped the conversation might embrace the future and not the past.

'Yes . . . it is.'

'I won't keep you. You'd best be on your way.'

'Good day to you, Mr. Halden.'

Mabel passed the bank and knew she had wanted to ask him about his son in the navy but wasn't sure how to without arousing Mr. Halden's suspicion. She envied Gertrude and all her soldier friends, and a navy lad would be just fine for her. Mabel had always shared her secrets and hopes for a relationship with Gertrude. Sometimes it was in the form of coded messages on postcards in the hope that their secrets would make it beyond the scrutiny of the those handling the post. Olive encouraged her closeness with Gertrude and laughed at any remarks relating to marriage plans. Louisa worked away *'trying to keep the wolf from the door'*, as she claimed, and felt that her daughters, now all over fourteen and Olive into her late twenties, were gradually escaping her control.

Mabel opened the door to the draper's shop.

So, Mr. Halden had family in Claydon. I wonder what Gertie's doing today. I must send her a card.

Back in the Square, William looked at the ivy-covered Castle House opposite, mulled over the coincidence, too, and went back to carrying crates.

Ada reflected on Mabel's news and stored it in the back of her mind. William wondered what she did with the information. He ruminated on the fact that Ada had formerly been a schoolteacher and one of her precepts was to save information for later use.

Ada had time for Mabel, too; her own sisters worked for drapers and dressmakers, so she was able to enter into Mabel's sphere. Ada had less time for Gertrude. She understood the bonds that tied the four sisters close together, knew they were very supportive of each other and shared very complementary personalities. They were happy.

Mabel, the youngest, was the only one left in the town centre now. Rose was in service some fifteen miles away, Olive on the other side of town, and Gertrude now in Claydon.

Ada thought she might catch Olive on a visit to Louisa's flat. There was no harm in asking after people, after all.

Chapter 18

Rose's first attack was barely over when she was caught up in another and collapsed on a visit to her mother. Louisa had dragged her as best as she could to her own bed. She sent an errand boy from the shop below to the doctor's.

When the doctor finally reached them, Rose opened two bleary eyes and, shivering, held on to the blankets.

'Thank you for coming so soon, Doctor.' said Louisa. 'She's poorly and has already had a bout of this recently. Feverish, too, with a rash.'

The doctor was fortunate enough to have already witnessed what he saw in the febrile frame of the young girl. It was most probably Lupus.

'Yes. This looks like something I saw last June. She'll need quinine, I think. Quinine, as you probably know, is used for malaria,' he said turning to Louisa. 'That should help her. It looks like what is known as Lupus. I'll write a prescription for you.'

The doctor studied the young girl's face where the rash had spread like two butterfly wings beneath her eyes. Clearly, she was exhausted, feverish and would need time to recover from the attack.

'What you have, Rose, is called Lupus and it will come and go for a very long time. You may have it all of your life, but you should be able to live with it providing you take rests, when necessary, and follow doctor's orders.'

The bedroom was bright, the wash basin stand and the mirror sat in their corner and a straggly cobweb on the windowpane caught her eye as Rose listened to the young doctor's words. She felt as if all of her limbs had caught fire and then once again the chill swept through her. The rattle of dray carts and the business of street conversations reached her window.

'I'm not sure she will be able to go back to work over the next twenty-four to forty-eight hours, Mrs. Harding.'

'Never mind, if it's for her own good, then that's all that matters, as far as I am concerned. Will Rose need to see her doctor in Broadmere, too?'

'I think it might be advisable. I will speak to him. I will be pleased to make his acquaintance.'

Rose lapsed into a slumber. Her mother's and the doctor's voices became a meaningless murmur.

* * *

The Avenue was full of sunlight and Ollie was standing at the gate wearing a white apron, the rustle of the elm trees was too loud for Rose to hear what she was saying. Ollie was joined by Nathalie and they both stood and beckoned Rose to approach the gate, but she couldn't breathe through her nose and every step was too slow. Her sister turned and went back into the house.

Louisa sat beside her. Her face close to hers. She ran her fingers through Rose's hair and wiped her forehead.

Rose drifted away again.

She chased and caught Timmy at the back of grand-

father's house and stroked his fur. Looking into the pond she saw the rippling reflection of the house and garden where the sisters listened to strains of the church organ as the married couple stepped forward and two lines of soldiers formed a guard of honor for the couple. Rose thought that Timmy was her only friend in life.

'We're not invited,' said Gertrude.

'We're not invited,' said Rose.

'We're not invited,' said Ollie.

She pulled at the white frill around the neck of her black dress, but it was tight and would not come away. The crepe material was too hot, and Gertie told her to kneel down for the photo, but Mabel had taken the black cat and she wanted the black cat. Then the children stood at the station gate holding hands as the steamer came into full view bearing the coffin and the policemen ordered the onlookers to keep back as the plume of smoke pulled the engine into view. Victoria to Victoria, Victoria to Victoria the onlookers kept saying. Infants Mabel and Bill were dressed in white robes and they both looked at her as Timmy escaped. Rose wanted to hold him but her nose was pinched and she couldn't breathe and her hands were slow and so she picked up the postcard instead and read 'Just think of me sitting here at home all alone but I'll make up for it on Wednesday I wonder what the matter was he was so quiet and seemed rather cross I was coming to see you but someone rather sharp caught me and was more punctual than usual now Gertrude is going away.'

* * *

Several days later the two doctors met.

'The girl's fortunate,' said Dr. Bradbury. 'Mrs. Tyndale's quick reaction was just in time and now her mother looking after her will be a boon.'

'Did you see the Lupus when she had her first attack?' asked Dr Witty.

'I wasn't sure, so I didn't prescribe anything apart from aspirin and rest. I thought she had a solid bout of influenza and the facial rash at that stage was not that pronounced.'

'Well, she survived . . . thank goodness. Anyway, as I was saying, Lupus Erythematosus may be attended by altogether more severe pathological changes. And, as we both know, that means '*dangerous constitutional symptoms may be intimately associated with the process*', and that, sadly, death may result from conditions arising from the local malady. Let's just hope that the quinine salicylate gets it under control. She's barely nineteen.'

'Yes, you're right. I may have been too dismissive of anything beyond the usual bout of influenza. I hear your point.'

Dr. Bradbury looked at the young Dr. Witty through his glasses and promised himself that he would keep an eye on Rose's welfare.

Chapter 19

To Olive, at least, Tom seemed debonair and charming. She thought his sweeping moustache certainly enhanced his young looks. He was learning his trade as a gunner and didn't spend much time on the subject with Olive; to her it was a very alien world. They enjoyed common friends and acquaintances and spent time in his village seated below the downs whenever he was given leave.

Tom's former trade as a carter had brought him many of these acquaintances and his friend, George, was still a drayman and accompanied the entire hop-picking to beer-brewing process and then took on its deliveries. His cart rumbled around the lanes and roads in and out of town carrying produce, hop baskets, beer barrels and crates. In September his cart ceremoniously bore the season's pickers from the railway station to the hop gardens. Both men had both grown up in this environment but now, whereas George still enjoyed the sounds and smells of his semi-rural occupation, Tom's senses were more accustomed to oil, coal-fired engine smoke, cordite, slamming turret hatches and exploding shells.

Tom and Olive came together naturally through friends, family, and work. Olive had seen the wreckage created by the death and disappearance of two fathers and the suffering of her mother and was under no illusion about the complications of married life. She was in no rush to settle down, but Tom's company, when available, was reassuring.

They stood on the platform with Mabel and mounted when the train pulled in. After slamming the doors and finding an empty compartment, they found themselves gazing at the countryside and fellow travellers as if time no longer had any hold on them and speech were of little use. Olive took Tom's arm.

Mabel was going to the shops with Olive and Tom was returning to the barracks for more training.

Mabel still thought a sailor would be best for her.

In Portsmouth the little group split up and the two sisters walked towards Southsea Common.

Olive rapped the brass doorknocker and a young woman opened and gazed first at one then at the other.

'Olive? What a surprise, come in!'

'This is my younger sister, May.'

'Hello, sweetheart,' said Lily. 'I am glad you both could come. I knew you had this Thursday off. What's more, I've got the house to myself. The cook and Mrs. Croft are out.'

Olive and Gertrude had known Lily Balm for number of years. Their paths had crossed in Southsea one afternoon, and they had started talking and later they shared a common reference: the workhouse. Lily had spent a year there, being discharged at the age of nine. Later she had made her way south as a very young girl in domestic service and was now employed by a lady. She was thirty-one.

While the three women stood on the doorstep, Mabel gazed back out at the seafront and she picked up the sound of the drag on the shingle as the waves receded and crashed again. The clear view over the stretch of water to the island captivated her.

Lily caught her gaze.

'If you want, we can go along the promenade and onto the pier.'

'I'd like that,' said Mabel.

Other walkers and passers-by caught up with them and overtook them as the three girls wandered to the pier, only recently re-opened after the fire. The chilly spring breeze caught their collars, bonnets and hair, and they stood at the railings agreeing that they were so lucky to live so close to the sea.

'Tom's gone back to the barracks, then he sails again,' said Olive. 'I don't know when he'll get leave.'

The waves collided with the stanchions below and sucked the shingle back into the sea.

'You know, Ollie, it's so different here. I hated London and everything that went on up there. Down here it's as if people led normal existences. Or rather, they actually have existences. You know, I wonder where a lot of us come from. I never knew my parents and just ended up in a Union Workhouse School, but got out quickly, and since then it has been anything but easy. Domestic service and more domestic service. One day maybe I'll meet someone to look after me.'

Olive watched the waves crash and recede and Mabel walked towards the end of the pier.

The drag on the shingle sounded powerful.

'Us women are all at a loss, it seems,' said Olive. 'And we're not the first. I think our mother's lost in a certain way, too. Two husbands that turned out badly and nothing but cleaning and more cleaning. But we're all in it, you know.'

'What do you mean? 'In it'.

'Well, there's not much else that we can do, is there? So, we just keep going, don't we? We'll never be rich.'

'Yes, I suppose so. But who is *it* all for? It's not really for us, is it?'

'Why not? I think we're happy enough. The Australians are good to me. They offer me both work and their friendship. We render them services; I do the housework, Nathalie cooks and cleans, too. It all works well. We have to look on the bright side, when we can, and I'm not sure the men have it better, either. By the way, Gertie's in London, you know.'

'I didn't actually, but it seemed she was going away to have the child.'

Olive looked at Mabel at the end of the pier.

'Well, it's due in June and she's in Claydon in some kind of Haven of Hope.'

'It's awful,' said Lily. 'How many babies end up lost to their real mothers and fathers? I mean, here I am not knowing myself really where I come from, and now Gertie's halfway to another fatherless baby. Does May know?'

'No, it's just as well. Nor do Rose or the boys. Mum's the word.'

Olive waited for Mabel as they halted by the newly rebuilt pavilion and wondered about the terrible conflagration of timbers, steel, fire and salt-water that had taken place a year ago.

Claydon

Chapter 20

'Are you coming?' asked Miss Amelia.

The post card brought news and a glimmer of happiness. Gertrude put it down and could still hear Olive's voice. She closed her door and looked out of the landing window over the church.

So, Tom back in the barracks, according to Ollie, and soon back at sea. She hoped Rose's work would not lead to her falling sick again and she was pleased to hear that her sisters had seen Lily.

Gertrude and other future young girl-mothers descended to the large white high-corniced front room overlooking the garden, the broad highway and the stately looking house on the other side. The large bay windows looked west just as the altar of the nearby church looked east.

A tramcar rattled by. Gertrude watched it.

Life's back to front, thought Gertrude.

Miss Amelia was about to lead the Bible class when an elderly man introduced himself. His forehead had a receding line of curly grey hair and he wore a shaggy beard in the Edwardian fashion. His eyes were dark. His voice took on a gentle timbre.

'Good afternoon to you all. My name is Ransom Willis and I would like to welcome those who are new to us and thank those who have returned to our Bible Class time and time again. As we know, the Lord moves in mysterious ways, but some of you follow his word and it is with much joy that we still see each other so regularly.'

He paused and looked benevolently at those he had not recognized.

'The Mission, thanks largely to Mrs. Willis, has been working for sixteen years and this year we hope to open our first full-scale maternity home and hospital. This beautiful house will be a haven of peace for you, no doubt, and I am sure you will feel safe and secure here. As you know and can see from the number of women with whom several of you are now acquainted, our mission grows greater by the day. We take in hundreds of girls, shelter and nurse them through their traumatic experiences. We also preach the Gospel of forgiveness, Christian sympathy and love.'

'Today my daughter will be taking the class and I do hope these classes will enable you to overcome your own apprehensions and feelings of guilt and despair.'

He stroked his beard and took a step backwards towards the door.

'Thank you, Amelia, and, once again, welcome.'

Mr. Willis left discreetly.

* * *

Amelia was reading the parable of the Good Samaritan when one of the girls raised her hand and asked her why the priest walked by on the other side of the road.

Miss Amelia looked out of the window and thought that the answer about a priest not being allowed to touch the dead was perhaps not fitting, for, according to the parable, the man was only half-dead.

At that moment she caught sight of three people standing on the pavement pointing at the house and the small sign. Their gesticulation and head shaking seemed to amount to thorough disapproval and incomprehension at the premises now used for other purposes than residence.

She changed her tack.

'The poor traveller was left for dead by the robbers and thieves as you know, and the priest and the Levite are not allowed to touch the dead, however, the Samaritan saw life where others saw death. He saw hope and could help where the others had just moved on because of their own limited worlds.'

She looked again at the small group outside now joined by a man in a hat and suit.

She started afresh.

'You know that man can be a terrible animal. He along with others can ignore, he can criticize, condemn and shame and he can lead the innocent to purgatory. And why? Because he is only interested in the purifying of sins and moral repair. His own self-righteousness is so enormous that he no longer sees the beam in his own eye.'

'What is self-righteousness?' asked the young girl sitting opposite her.

Amelia paused.

'It's when you think that you, your beliefs and your way of life, shall we say, are better and holier than those of others.'

'Thank you,' said the girl.

'But we have sinned, haven't we?' asked Gertrude. 'So, shouldn't we ask for forgiveness?

Amelia looked into Gertrude's eyes.

'Gertrude, why do you say that you have sinned?'

'I suppose, because that's the way people see it and how I see it, too.'

'So, you are prey to others whose moral values and sense of condemnation have no room for forgiveness, sympathy, or love. You see, you too, fall foul of the self-righteous. However, values such as forgiveness, sympathy or love are those that you, no doubt, esteem highly.'

Gertrude nodded.

'Some girls have come here pregnant with a second child and we do not turn them away. Outside, those girls would become scapegoats for many, harried and chased from pillar to post with nowhere to go, but at the same time fulfilling the terrible need for all those who gratify their own righteousness, because they . . . they have not fallen so low, that is, so low in their own eyes. That alone enables them to feel completely vindicated in their condemnation of others.'

'But I feel I *have* fallen low,' said Gertrude.

'That's only natural. Most of our values are inherited from our family and those of our immediate environment, Gertrude. These may be tired and worn values, which may no longer apply today. Values that have been bandied about just as much as proverbs and moral codes. Some true values weather the changes of season and remain, others disappear.'

Amelia took time to look at all the girls in the group and sensed that she was on difficult ground. Some girls may not be able to follow at all.

The girl that Gertrude had met a few days ago on her arrival raised her hand.

'Miss Amelia, are you saying that our parents and our friends are responsible for us being in this way with child?'

'I am saying that there are many truths out there,' she pointed at the little group still present on the pavement, 'and you must find the truth which will lead you away from the torment that you suffer today.'

She turned to Gertrude again.

'You held the soldier you loved in your heart, didn't you? Was it a first love?'

'Yes.'

'And where is that man now?'

'I don't know. I think he may be in Ireland.'

'And does he still have a place in your heart?'

Gertrude turned her head and looked at the girl who had been told she should find the truth to ease her torment.

'I can't say 'no', and ultimately the child will be ours. I feel it's all so confusing. I'm sorry.'

Amelia felt that the time had come to conclude.

'Thank you all. Thank you, Gertrude, for your last remark. Forgiveness is the path of righteousness. Some of you have been here a little longer than Gertrude and I would appreciate it, if you could help her through the coming days and weeks. Please use your Bibles and think about the following lines from the Book of Isaiah.'

He was despised and rejected by mankind, a man of suffering, and familiar with pain. Like one from whom people hide their faces he was despised, and we held him in low esteem.

'We shall talk about them tomorrow.'

* * *

The fair weather was enticing. Gertrude pulled the front door open and wandered along the road towards the broad green with the little lake. Others followed her. She looked for rowing boats but saw none.

Chapter 21

Early in June Gertrude was enormously pregnant and could hardly move. Three months of cooking, gardening, helping with other mothers had gradually subsided as Gertrude had found it harder by the day. She sensed the birth had to be today. The contractions had started during the night and, although bearable, she knew they could only become more powerful. She was worried. Worried that the pain would be too much for her and that something might happen to the child. She looked at the four walls and the view over the plain garden at the back. The church clock struck eight and Laura, dressed in a white apron, marched into the room.

'Good morning, Gertrude. Are you in pain?'

Gertrude felt clumsy, tired and lost and wished the contractions would cease.

'I think it won't be long now. I've been getting regular contractions and they're more and more painful.'

All of a sudden, she doubled up. A giant wave of contraction, like a giant leather belt, took hold of her midriff and she clutched at the bed rails and breathed almightily. Sweat ran down her face and Laura waited for the moment to pass. Gertrude closed her eyes and gritted her teeth thinking somebody had just blasted her entrails.

Laura examined Gertrude and went downstairs for help. Fortunately, Gertrude had entered into labour before Daisy, who had also suffered overnight. Laura would now be devoted to Gertrude.

Gertrude gasped and lay still. She knew she was safe here. The sympathy and love provided by the Mission and the hours of talking about forgiveness and Christian values had found their place in Gertrude's heart. She was fine here, she said to herself as another tremendous spasm caught her unexpectedly and she writhed with the pain.

She heard Laura on the stairs and called.

'Please, Laura. Quick.'

Laura hurried into the room with another girl in attendance carrying bundles.

'Do the breathing, Gertie,' she said.

Gertrude's body split in two and all three women heard the first plaintive cry.

The church bell sounded again. Gertrude gradually regained her breath and felt the small body wrapped in towelling resting on her.

'Not even time to get to the Mayday,' said Laura. 'Just as well there were no complications. It's a boy, Gertie.'

'Hello, sweetheart,' Gertrude said and held the baby close. She shut her eyes while calm seemed to be restored for a few minutes.

Gertrude sensed it was just the beginning of a very different ordeal.

How was she going to deal with this little bundle as he lay on her and opened his blue eyes? Within moments the child would be suckling and then in the days ahead the dreadful prospect of weaning would be the signal of their last moments together.

* * *

Two days later in Maydurham Olive received a cryptic message and knew that her sister needed her.

The wind caught the elms in the Avenue and in the distance the lake started to ripple.

She turned the key in the lock at 'Cossington', placed the shopping in the kitchen and mounted the stairs. Nathalie caught her as she reached the landing. The two women stood in silence and Nathalie beckoned Olive into her room. She evidently wished to share something that should not be overheard.

'I had a strange encounter in town,' she said.

Olive undid the bows on her hat and placed it on the chair. She was puzzled by Nathalie's tone.

'I was at the market and I met Ada from the pub . . . she asked me about you and your sisters. She seemed particularly interested in Gertie. I felt she was insisting.'

Olive sighed and wondered what she could say. Keeping Nathalie out of the picture seemed the right way to proceed, despite the intimacy that the young women shared. Nathalie was a close friend, but Gertrude's predicament was a serious worry for her and Louisa. Olive had only confided in Lily. She knew that Lily had so many terrible secrets of her own to keep that she could trust her. Lily was also out of town.

'Why?' What do you mean by 'insisting'?

'Well, she said that Gertrude had left the Lewis sisters to go and work in Claydon. She said that was quite a change in scenery . . . I don't know, it just felt that she was fishing for news.'

‘It is quite a change, but the sisters have been very kind to Gertrude, and they needed somebody to help them with a friend’s boarding house in Claydon, so Gertie volunteered.’

‘So, when did she go?’

‘Two months ago.’

‘You never said anything. Nor did Gertie.’

‘You were in Flanders when she left.’

‘Oh, yes. I remember now.’

Olive breathed in; she knew that she was only lying partially. The Mission resembled a boarding house and Gertrude was involved in cleaning, cooking and gardening, too. That Gertrude had not volunteered and that she was expecting were the only facts to hide.

‘When will she be back?’

‘I’ve no idea, I am sure she’ll let us know soon. I think she said September.’

Nathalie hurried back down to the kitchen and Olive picked up her housecoat. As she changed, she thought that they had already suffered enough from their stepfather first being confined to prison and then to the workhouse, and that the whole ordeal had already taken a long time to fade from the looks and encounters with other townsfolk. If Gertrude’s secret escaped to the High Street gossips, then the family might just as well try to move elsewhere.

When her stepfather’s fate had been made public, Olive hardly knew where the terrible pressure on the family had come from. Was it the family’s own sense of discredit and shame, or the tangible spread of idle gossip and curious looks which hurt the most?

She had always kept herself to herself. Family circumstances dictated. She kept her head down and ploughed on.

The brothers would never be affected as much as the sisters, and now the most joyous of the four had been snared by a soldier, Rose had health worries and May needed watching. Their true friends would support them and understand, but beyond those friends, other persons' behaviour was typeset and channeled by convention. Thinking differently existed but acting differently had not yet come to stay. Would her mother, Gertrude and herself find it difficult to maintain their jobs, if their reputation was tarnished a second time, she wondered.

She put her hand into her apron pocket. A post card had come for her earlier in the day.

She read the text again.

> *'Dear sister thanks for your PC it was good to know you are still seeing Lily give her my love I hope Rose is better. My job here will now be finishing in the coming weeks. I hope you will be able to come up before then to see us. Your ever loving sister, Gertie.'*

Going to Claydon struck her as logical. Tom wouldn't need to know, either.

Portsmouth

Chapter 22

Tom had returned to *HMS Commonwealth* currently under the orders of Horace Hood. He and Olive had become accustomed to their stop-go relationship. Caring for each other in Maydurham or when separated was their aim for the time being.

The training he had undergone as a Royal Marine in the Artillery destined him to the shafts and hoists for shells and cordite and the gun turrets above. In the mechanized world of modern navies, *HMS Commonwealth* was a pre-*Dreadnought* and thus superseded by the engineering of the latest vessels. It would be due for a refit within the next two years. For two years it was his ship, his navy, his waves and his life. Both he and his shipmates looked upon the remarkable hull and Captain Horace Hood as a sea-borne home, a knitted and coordinated community. The association between the body of men and their destiny passed through the orders, the day-to-day occupation of drills, exercises, and the care of the ship and its seaworthiness in readiness for engagement. The ships were deemed invulnerable with their layers of steel and numerous bulkheads, colossal twelve-inch guns and steam turbines.

Now in his late twenties, Tom had not seen action, having spent time in the Mediterranean, the Channel and on the Irish coast engaged in his subaltern role below decks, a barely visible but vital part of the minutiae of Britannia's control of the seas where thousands of young men and boys entertained the glory of Nelson's fleet and hoped one day to emulate their predecessors whenever the time would arise.

Subconsciously it was as if the crews and commanders had begun their preparations in expectation of *'Der Tag'* when the two largest fleets would fight to their death. The artillery training, the patrols, the new intensity in the production of *Dreadnoughts* were the seemingly logical steps of a nation heading for the battle of all battles where the enemy would be wiped out once and for all. The race for superiority had set in and knowing where it would lead, or when its climax would come, was still a dim concept.

Tom descended to the mess deck and found himself opposite Gunners Barrett and Beeston. They had spent the morning greasing and checking the hoists.

'So today they want us to check all the hoists and tomorrow they'll take them out and replace them with even faster and more complicated hoists and when they jam, the engineers will have to learn how to repair those. It's a never-ending race for improvement,' Barrett groaned. 'Today it's Dreadnoughts, tomorrow it's super-Dreadnoughts.'

'And when the breach load is too slow, we end up with extra cordite canisters in the gun turret,' Beeston said musingly, not really following the flow of the conversation.

'It's all very well when you're working on the training ship, but you try doing the same in a raging sea or even calm sea with the rock from the enemy splashes, it ain't exactly the same,' said Tom. 'Plus, the time it takes to get a range in those conditions. All right, they're using the Dreyer to give us a simpler task, you know, 'aim at the mark and fire' . . . but straddling the enemy takes time and a bit of luck, too.'

'How's the ears, Tom?' Barrett asked.

'They come and go, you know. Cotton wool does the trick but only for a while. Bloody nuisance really.'

'The boom and the recoil, you know, in the twelve-inchers, well, it's frightening, when you come to think about it. Some people just end up bleeding from their ears,' Beeston added.

'Happy fellow, aren't you, Stan?' Tom commented.

The men had been told of the risks and perils of war but none of it was particularly real. Their reality was range finding, firing and upping their firing rate, drills and putting out to sea to practice again.

George Barrett remembered a story he had heard:

'Talking of engagements, I've got a mate who's sailed under Packenham, you know, the captain of *HMS Antrim*, and he overheard what Packenham had said about his time as observer with the Japanese in the war with the Russians.

'He was standing on the foredeck of this Japanese battleship with his binoculars when shrapnel from a Russian shell just missed him but mutilated and massacred the Japanese crewmen nearby and he was just covered in body parts and blood. So, all he did was to go to his cabin and change into his best whites and come back to carry on observing.

'Then later on he saw one of the Russian battleships low in the water, I think it was the *Borodino,* which hadn't yet gone down, and the Japs were pulling out because the

Russians had basically had it, but one of them fired off a last couple of twelve-inchers in the *Borodino's* direction and next thing you know the gun-turret's blown off, the ammunition's alight and the cordite fire goes straight down to the magazines, so within minutes the ship just explodes leaving one survivor. All gone, eight hundred and fifty men just like that . . . in a whiff.'

'Thanks for the good news, George,' retorted Tom. 'But then it's a chance in how many for a strike like that?'

'I can't say but it's probably shorter odds than you'd imagine.'

For a moment the men sat in silence.

Barrett looked at his colleagues.

'They say it was the turning-point. You know, the Japanese won the war and so our worries about our colonies in the East were safe. We supported the Japanese and the Russian threat fizzled out. Now all we seem to worry about is Germany, Germany, Germany.'

'When's the big day, Tom?' Stan interrupted.

'Big day? You mean me and Olive? . . . Well, I don't know, but I reckon if we're still going serious in a year's time, why not? Being married to a sailor isn't exactly easy and I don't know if that's what Olive really wants.'

Claydon

Chapter 23

A week later Gertrude found herself breast-feeding the little face that looked up to her craving for more. When she had finished, the child was finally sated, quiet and contented. It was always at this moment when Gertrude felt the trap and anguish build around her. Her own flesh and blood was to become the possession of a person or persons she would never meet and never know. Time seemed to be running out and while she clutched the child here and now, she felt that it was all she had ever wanted. Outside, the world had other plans and papers to sign, which would sever their tie and leave her with heartbreak and regret, a passport into the next days of her life. She had an appointment with Mrs Willis.

Laura came into Gertrude's room and offered to take baby Freddie whilst Gertrude readied herself.

'He's a bonny little fellow,' she said. 'He's a fair size.'

Gertrude looked at her child in Laura's arms.

'I think I may ask for foster care later,' she said almost inquiringly.

Laura picked up on her tone of voice and said that it was perhaps half of a solution, which would enable Gertrude to receive news in the meantime and continue to entertain the idea of taking him home, should the possibility arise. There would be a payment but at least the child would be cared for by the Mission for a certain time before that. Freddie would be in the Boy's Home until then.

* * *

Gertrude walked up the drive to the large house again. It was only the second time. Miss Hurd appeared at the door and beckoned her to come into the hall and wait a few minutes. She again caught sight of the now recognisable Bible-studies books.

Miss Amelia had worked hard with their groups and, thanks to her, Gertrude knew that she was a protected and respected part of a community which had a different path in life from that of so many other women with regular families. The Mission's community had embraced her as she was and, despite her 'mistake', their message was that life would still buoy her up and ensure that the best was done for her and her baby.

She knew that full well, but still wondered on the actual meaning of the word 'best'.

Was 'best' just a means of turning the abnormal into the normal by some form of persuasion where Jesus acted as the medium? The Bible Study classes had given her that impression. She was so afraid of the coming days. She knew she had failed and that her die was cast and she would not be able to ignore the looks of others.

Mrs. Willis stood in her doorway and smiled at Gertrude. Then she beckoned her to come in and take a seat. Gertrude took in the new proverbs that hung on the wall. '*It is love that keeps the world warm*' now had competition. She surveyed the usual darkened recesses of the room and the piles of documents, and, once seated, held herself upright as if expecting a verdict.

'I believe I know what you are thinking Gertrude. So many girls come here after the birth of their baby and find themselves in the same state of mind.'

'Good afternoon Mrs. Willis. Thank you. I must admit that the coming weeks seem to be a fearful prospect and I have so much love for the baby.'

'Then we must lay your fears to rest.' Miss Willis replied. 'Getting on after an ordeal of this kind is a long process. As Amelia has told you in her classes with you, only one or two stories can make sense in this difficult world, and you must remember them . . . they can and will give you strength. The number of birth mothers we look after never dwindles and each one requires care and attention and a great deal of reassurance. Some girls find their feet because they put matters behind them quickly and others sink back into terrible sadness. So much is linked to the very nature of the person in their survival from this ordeal. Maybe, I am being too general but . . . well . . . perhaps, Miss Hurd, you would like to tell Gertrude about Doris.'

Miss Hurd started on a story about one of the young mothers who had spent her time at the Mission and was facing the prospect of going back into the outside world to try to find work whilst leaving behind her four-month-old child.

'You know, Gertrude, when Doris left, she came to see us and asked if a particular charge-nurse would kiss her baby daughter every day at bedtime, because she had red-hair like Doris. That way the baby would think that her mother was still there.'

Gertrude looked about the room and counted the weeks and wondered if any of the charge-nurses or matrons had unmanageable wiry curls like her.

'You will understand, Gertrude, that the story is rather sad, but I think that what it expresses is the faith that you must have in the Mission and in those who work with the children. You have already seen the example set by the charge-nurses and Laura's devotion at London Road where Freddie will be looked after, and you can follow his progress. Miss Hurd will reply to all of your correspondence and you can make your decision about foster care or adoption when the baby is a little older. The babies become their own community and grow up together in many cases. When it is time for schooling, they are given a proper education.'

The future of her child was rolled out before her.

It seemed safe. It seemed organized. It seemed healthy. It resembled a boarding school from the cradle to adolescence.

Gertrude remembered the boarding school in her town and began to wonder how those boys could just be left there by naval families whilst the parents lived out their own lives and collected their sons at the end of term. The parents were married, and the child was not illegitimate. Wasn't that even more morally reprehensible than her predicament? The only saving grace for those parents was the unchanging surname and the ongoing correspondence until the boy moved into a profession or one of the services.

She could write, too, but if he were to be adopted, then his surname name would change, the link to an abode would disappear from view and every waking minute of

Gertrude's current ordeal would be unheard of and irrelevant to the adoption family. The slate would be wiped clean and the ties between her and Freddie severed forever.

On this particular score, however, Gertrude had no idea that the Mission was operating beyond the bounds of the law.

'Thank you, Miss Willis. I cannot part with him like that and I would really wish him to be here where I know the people and the Mission. I will pay you for the year and I do hope that one day Freddie and I will be reunited. I would like to spend a few more weeks with him.'

'As you wish, Gertrude, but please remember that weaning is already hard enough under normal circumstances, perhaps, it is unwise to prolong too much.'

Mrs. Willis's Mona Lisa-like face was a mixture of understanding and gentle looks, and all the while firm and reassuring. It came from her matronly physique and the wisdom that seemed to emanate from her grey hair and broad forehead.

'How many desperate girls has she helped?' thought Gertrude. 'I must be just one of hundreds.'

'My sister has offered to come to Claydon in the next few days. Is that all right with you, Mrs. Willis?'

'Of course, I shall make it my duty to meet her, too. You are a lucky girl, Gertrude. As you have already told me, you actually have a family to care for you, too.'

Chapter 24

Olive arrived towards the end of June when baby Fred was barely three weeks old. She wandered up the long London Road in the heat of the day. The size of the town, if measured by the interminable walk compared to the short distances she travelled around Maydurham, left her with a sense of awe for the areas of Greater London. She finally found Gertrude's dwellings, looked out at the mansion opposite and thought that the area was a sedate and refined South London borough. Nevertheless, the hustle and bustle of the errand boys, horses and traps, and clanging of trams just emphasized the rush of human activity and the disappearance of time. To Olive this was a stark contrast with the parochial environment of her hometown where her fellow townsfolk seemed to be able measure out and control their time.

She had dreaded this trip but had taken it upon herself to help her sister. At the same time, she knew her visit was possibly just a palliative for the traumatic impending separation of mother and child. The thought of holding that small child only to know he may never be theirs drained her soul. After all the innocent and fun postcards the sisters had sent back and forth about thoughts of marriage, finding a man and building a family, Gertrude's fortune had spiralled out of control until she'd become a 'fallen woman.'

As Olive looked at the splendid house, she reflected on

the future environment her sister would return to. It would not be simple.

Although only Louisa, Olive, and the Lewis sisters knew of Gertrude's predicament, Gertrude's absence had not gone unnoticed in Maydurham. Ada had recently met Olive in the square and seemed to concentrate much of the conversation on the fact that Claydon was where her parents-in-law had lived not so long ago and that she hoped Gertrude's work for the Lewis sisters' acquaintances was going well. Olive knew this was more than idle conversation. Ada was testing, not out of malevolence because the two families were acquainted, but she was testing, nonetheless.

Olive knew that looks wore more of a meaning than words and had steadied her gaze on Ada in an attempt to shield any hint of dishonesty. She was perspicacious and honest, knowing full well she found it an ordeal to summon up even white lies to protect her family. The warnings, nevertheless, were there. Even if Ada's interest had been benign, any doubtful information passed onto the curious and ill-natured would soon conspire to drive suspicion about Gertrude's journey and stay. The excuse of temporary service in a boarding house would wear thin. Olive imagined the looks in the street, the turning of heads, and the audible whispers that would soon be manifest. Gertrude would have to remain discreet for some time and the Lewis sisters would be enlisted to help by keeping her in their employ and lodging her away from the town centre.

Her father's committal had already brought enough shame upon the family.

She knocked on the elegant door of number 240 London Road and was let in by a young and handsome woman in her nurse's uniform who went by the name of 'Laura'. She asked Olive to wait a second and called Gertrude.

'She's been expecting you. She's happy you decided to come.'

'Thank you kindly,' said Olive as she removed her bonnet and looked at the rather stately staircase which rose directly before her. She turned her head and caught sight of the large white and airy front room she had first noticed from the road. Chairs were set out as if for some kind of meeting, and painted biblical figures as well as hand-written verses on large cards lent against the bottom of a large bookcase. Olive noticed the painting of the *Good Samaritan;* the traveller held up the dying man's head and gave him water.

Laura noticed Olive's gaze.

'We have Bible reading classes here, to try to enable the mothers to get over their terrible feelings of guilt. Miss Willis runs them. They help. The birth of children from unwanted pregnancies is daunting and an everlasting trauma. The women here need more than clinical help. Some will never be able to face their families and friends ever again. Miss Willis doesn't try to evangelize, but stories like these provide a form of moral strength. She does a lot with the Mission's nursery, too, where baby Frederick will probably go. I think that's what Gertrude wants.'

At that moment Gertrude appeared from the kitchen.

'Ollie,' she smiled.

Olive looked at her younger sister and tried to imagine the mixture of feelings she must be going through: a mother and a new baby, neither with a future.

'Oh, my. Gertie, how lovely to see you.'

Gertrude took her arm and led her up the staircase.

'Let me show you Freddie,' she said.

The sisters stood by the cot as the child stirred. Gertrude picked him up gave him to Olive.

'Do you breast feed?'

'Yes, it's such a joy.'

Olive gazed into his blue eyes as he turned his head left and right and opened his little mouth with its gentle gums. He searched for a breast.

'He sleeps quite a lot at night now and seems to have got into a rhythm. I feed him first thing in the morning and do some work in the kitchen after, while he sleeps. Laura looks in on him. I *am* lucky, Ollie.'

Olive wasn't sure that 'lucky' was really what Gertrude intended but today, here and now, her sister had found a certain serenity even if it was merely a false dawn. Gertrude had meant that now the soldier and father had vanished from the scene, she had one objective in life for which she was glad: the welfare of this tiny being. In her current environment everything was there to help her until the day they separated mother and child. Olive wished that day would never come and watched her sister as she busied herself with the little being in its nappies and cotton sleeveless undergarments.

She handed Gertrude a little package. 'Mother knitted them for you.'

Gertrude found a pair of woollen boots and a little woollen coat.

'They're beautiful. Tell mother from me, please.'

Olive stopped herself from saying she had had to buy the wool in Portsmouth.

She changed tack.

'So, you do Bible readings?

'Yes, Miss Willis is very good. Then we talk about our own experiences. It's not easy, though. I mean . . . when I see what some of the girls are going through, I count myself as lucky. But the stories are all very much the same. One girl called, Irene, was left standing at the altar by her soldier man and never saw him again. Miss Willis told us stories about some of the children in the boys' house, too.

In one she said she was attending ping-pong games with some of the boys and one child asked where he really lived. She told him he really lived there in the boys' house in Hirst Road. But he replied:

'I don't mean that. Where do I *really* live?'

Gertrude paused.

'So, you see, Ollie, even when they are very young, they know, they know . . .'

Gertrude looked out of the window into the distance where nothing could really be seen apart from the wall of the house, the garden and the rear of the church. She wiped her eyes.

'The Bible readings,' said Gertrude. 'Yes, they give us a sort of peace of mind and strength, but it's just for a period and then the world seems to return to normal. I really don't know what to do, Ollie.'

'The nurse said you would probably like baby Freddie to be brought up here. That sounds reasonable to start with. I think they care well for the children.'

Gertrude looked up slightly reassured.

'I know they do. He won't want for food and comfort I am sure,' she said. 'Maybe I will be able to help him from afar. It will be a cost, too. But I will do all I can to support him as long as necessary.'

Olive knew her sister was determined. Maybe this determination would carry her though the trauma of separation.

The sisters put the child back in the cot and descended to the front gate where they stood and wondered why they were both there in a strange town with unrecognisable landmarks and a loss of bearings. Even the large imposing edifice and front lawn opposite held out nothing but a sense of abstraction. Only the little heartbeat in a second-floor bedroom cut through the absurd.

'Mrs. Willis said she would like to meet you, Ollie, but I don't know that it's the right thing. I think I have to do all this myself.'

They embraced and Olive took her leave and walked towards the railway station wishing that she could put the clocks back three or four years.

Gertrude watched the back of her sister, her beloved mentor, until she could no longer distinguish her among the pedestrians.

I have now set the family a new ordeal that will sap the morale of those who know. They will never be able to cope with it easily. I just hope that Rose and May never stumble like me. Perhaps, somehow, it would be better if they actually knew.

* * *

Six weeks later Gertrude found herself on the train heading south, her suitcase beside her.

'Just my suitcase and my bonnet.'

The train steamed on, then halted. Doors slammed and

voices called out. Another station and yet another. She was going home. It was all she could do. Her family would meet her on the platform.

Maydurham

Chapter 25

During that last week of July an afternoon train steamed into the station and passengers clambered out. It was on its way down to the coast: Portsmouth Harbour. There was an air of summer travel about the arrival of the train; the porters pushed their way forward and collected trunks and parcels from the goods van.

The idea of summer travel was lost on Gertrude as she stood at the southern end of the platform, surveying the scene. She headed back up to the familiar station exit where Olive and her mother stood. She looked about, hoping there would be no acquaintances or familiar shopkeepers.

The small party embraced and took the usual route over the crossing, making their way towards the Wincaster road. The route enabled them to avoid townsfolk in and around the main station entrance and consequently the potential for triggering gossip.

Louisa told Gertrude she looked well but was ill-prepared to say more. Ollie offered to carry her case.

The little group soon passed under the railway bridge and turned into the green lane towards Gertrude's former dwelling. The heat of the day under the bluish sky was bearable and the fields, the bushes, the grazing cattle and the distant hangers were the setting for the three women as they stood before the boarding house.

A passer-by would have said that every picture tells a story. Every picture with its frame is the fiction and the occupants only play to the imagination of the viewer, but here, in this picture, the viewer would have been lost, for the faces were hidden and only their backs and the suitcase were visible as they looked up at the house and then at the gate leading into the field. *'It was a moment of hesitation,'* the passer-by might have said. *'A moment of anxiousness,'* another might have surmised, and yet neither would have been able to account for the thoughts running through Gertrude's mind. They were unutterable.

She looked at Olive and they stepped into the courtyard before ringing the doorbell.

'Gertrude!' Lily Alice said happily as she opened the door. 'It's so lovely to see you again.'

Gertrude smiled and tried to find a semblance of self-control.

It was true, though, she was glad to see Lily Alice again.

'I will just get Miss Annie. Miss Marie is away for a few days.'

The family were ushered into the large front room with its bay window and view over the field and downs.

'Don't worry Gertie,' said Olive.

Her mother said nothing, and they waited for the footsteps in the hall.

'Thank you, Lily Alice.' said Miss Annie and she shut the front room door and seated herself with the little group.

'How are you Gertrude? I know it's not the right question, but we must start somewhere. Please tell me.'

She didn't know that she had asked the question that preoccupied Louisa and Olive just as much. The question they had uncharacteristically been unable to ask.

'Well, I said 'goodbye' to him this morning and now he's gone, and I am gone.'

Gertrude realised that 'saying goodbye' was a dreadful euphemism for the depth of sorrow she had felt. She crushed her handkerchief into the palm of her hand. The anguish on her face resonated on the looks of the three others.

'I am sure that must have been a dreadful ordeal,' Miss Lewis replied, merely stating the obvious. There was nothing else.

'It was and I wouldn't wish it on anyone.'

Olive seemed motivated to say something and Miss Lewis noticed.

'Yes, Olive?'

'If you don't mind my saying, Miss Lewis, Gertrude has left baby Frederick with the Mission and she wants him to grow up there so that she can care for him at a distance rather than wish him to be lost through adoption.'

'Well, that must make you feel you are still in contact some way or another with him?' Miss Lewis replied.

'Maybe,' said Gertrude. 'There is one thing I haven't told you and that is baby Freddie actually has your name as his middle name. He's called Frederick Lewis Kimble. I wanted him to be called after you after all your kindness to me.'

Annie Lewis heard the words and looked out of the window. Her eyes glistened. She paused and turned to Gertrude

'Thank you, Gertrude. I don't know what to say. I am so touched. My sister will be so pleased, too.' She looked away again and then asked: 'Can we count on you to work for us again, Gertrude?'

'Yes. Of course, I owe you so much already. Thank you.'

Olive and Louisa shifted in their seats. This was a moment of great relief. The family had made its way out of so many scrapes thanks to the kindness of people around them, yet Gertrude's worries back in her hometown had really only just begun again. They expected a bumpy ride and it would be necessary to keep Gertrude out of the town itself as much as possible.

Gertrude seemed to have acknowledged their thoughts and asked Miss Annie if she could use her former bedroom, thus remaining discreetly away from the usual hubbub of the townsfolk.

'Of course, Gertrude. We will do our best to keep you out of the way until you find it easier to mix with people. What's more, there's a lot of work to be done looking after our boarders. Your room is ready for you. If you would like to settle in, we can then deal with the new arrivals for this evening.'

The Lewis sisters had wanted Gertrude to be occupied as soon as possible to keep her mind off her dreadful separation as much as could be feasible.

Olive and Louisa stood and thanked Miss Annie for the two sisters' generosity. They said they would take Gertrude to the foot of her stairs and then return home. Gertrude still had so much to tell and yet Miss Annie and her family seemed more intent on letting her get on. Perhaps, they thought that she was strong enough to cope.

* * *

Gertrude kept herself to herself but confided in the two sisters now and then. She explained her stay in Claydon and in particular the moments spent with other expectant mothers, Mrs. Willis, Miss Hurd, and Miss Amelia, as well as the Christian morals and parables they talked about so much. They had kept her from sinking into a despondency that she feared she would never have been able to emerge from.

As hours grew into days, the separation from Freddie hit her time and time again. The sisters had been supportive and helpful since her return. But she caught herself staring into space and the space seemed occupied by one thing only; that last touch and embrace before coming home.

Home was the wrong word. Home was being with her child.

In the last days of autumn Mary Lewis saw Gertrude with a letter in her hand. As she was on her way to the post office, she offered to take the letter for Gertrude. Gertrude hesitated slightly. Normally her letters or cards just went into the red box at the end of the road thus enabling her to avoid contact with curious passers-by. She handed the letter to Miss Lewis.

Having glanced at the address Mary Lewis saw Gertrude was sending a letter to the Mrs. Willis.

'What's the news of Freddie?' she asked.

'He's well, I believe.'

'Does Miss Hurd send you much news?'

'Yes, but I have the impression that she writes the same letter to all the mothers.'

'I see. Are you able to keep up with your payments?'

'Well, I have given them £25 for his upkeep until February and then I will have to send some more money.

But at least I have his custody and he is being looked after. I just wish . . .'

'Yes, Gertrude.' said Miss Lewis. 'We all would wish the same for you. I will put this in the post in town.'

'Thank you, Miss Lewis.'

She watched Miss Lewis move down the lane between the bare trees, hedgerow and field. She envisaged the next few months or years as a means of retreat to a haven of safety or spiritual sanctuary where she could care for her baby son from a distance. She knew that she was no longer the fun-loving and rather carefree person she had been more than a year ago. Life was different and so was she.

* * *

Ten months after the birth of her child and more than a year after her move to Claydon, the housekeeper, Lily Alice, handed Gertrude a post card. The picture showed a cherub with her bow. The caption box indented with the forms of hearts ran:

True love is like unto a ticklish sensation in the regions of the heart which cannot be scratched. But I have heard there is a cure.

Gertrude turned the card over. It came from Dublin.

I hope you will like this postcard. Should very much like one in return for old times' sake. CHS.

Chapter 26

Olive and Tom married in July, a Thursday at 2:30 pm, exactly two years after Gertrude's return to Maydurham.

The church marriage was attended by a large party of family and friends. The abundance of flowered hats brought a tremendously festive tone to the modest couple's union. They brought their guests to the reception hall and circulated amongst them. Olive was made for marriage and, for once, without her customary about-town bonnet seemed like a different person. Mabel had helped make Olive's dress with materials from her shop. Tom wore his uniform and impressed Louisa who was so proud. Brothers Fred and Bill had escaped their work and found themselves in pleasant company. Lily had come from Portsmouth. Gertrude and the Lewis sisters also formed a small group.

It was in many ways a double celebration. After years of a rather forlorn existence in the shadows of two departed fathers, the family had suddenly been buoyed up by Fred's marriage to Emily as well as the birth of their first child just days before Olive's wedding. Fred's wife was in her twentieth year and the fact was not lost on Gertrude. The contrast in good fortune, happiness and circumstances played on her mind and Olive found her in her usual reverie.

'You do look lovely, Ollie. It's such a wonderful day,' she said. 'Tom looks smart and happy.'

'Thanks, Gertie.'

Emily and her baby found a seat nearby.

Olive understood the dawning look on Gertrude's face but could not help saying:

'Baby boy, Leslie. I wonder where Fred got that name. 'He's still given him 'Frederick' as his middle name though.'

Gertrude wished that she could stop everybody calling their children by the name 'Frederick'.

'How long is Tom off for?'

'Just a few days and then back to the barracks.'

'I hope the weather stays nice for you on the Isle of Wight.'

Olive and Tom would catch the train later that evening to spend a weekend in Ryde. It seemed exotic and different, just because of the ferry ride across the Solent. It also conjured up visions of royalty.

'I do too,' said Olive. 'We may try and catch a bus to Osborne House and catch up with George.'

'Ha, ha,' said Gertrude. 'Still, if the Isle of Wight's good enough for them, then you've made the right choice.'

'Funny, isn't it?' quipped Olive.

'What's that?'

'That we might be on our way to visit a royal family of Germanic descent with a British sailor training to defend the seas against their cousins. The world's back to front!'

Gertrude laughed and Olive said it wasn't right for women to be political.

'It's not right for us to be a whole lot of things,' said Gertrude. She looked around for listeners and went on: 'I know I mustn't complain, but that's part of the problem. We are not even supposed to complain. I feel I have to keep hold of such a dreadful secret that just gnaws away at me day in day out, and just grin and bear it. '*Never complain, never explain*'. That's what the man said, wasn't it? So now we have to button our bottom-lip and bow. Sorry, Olive, it's your wedding and I am getting carried away.'

'Let's go and speak to Lily,' Olive suggested. 'She's getting married soon, too.'

'Yes, I know, she told me on the way into the registry office.'

Lily was holding a cup of tea and looking elegant in her grey dress and bonnet. Her hair was brushed back and held in a bun, something Gertrude would never be able to do. She had started a conversation with Rose.

'How are you dealing with your Lupus, Rose?'

'Well, thanks. It comes and goes but the quinine works. Thanks for your card the other day.'

'It's my pleasure.'

'You know the albums and the family, sometimes I feel like it's almost as if the they're vital to everybody's existence. I suppose they will be one day when we've all disappeared!' she said with a great big half-moon grin.

Lily smiled and then Gertrude intruded. Rose said she would fetch more tea.

'Have you got *your* date yet?' asked Gertrude.

'Yes, it's a Wednesday. The 20th of September. David will be able to get away for a day or two, that's all. A bit like Tom. I wanted Olive and Tom as witnesses, but they can't get leave that easily. Once in the services, always in the services.'

David McCormack was a gunner in the Garrison Artillery. When they met, Tom and David laughed about their artillery links. 'I pass them and he fires them,' was their party piece.

Rose was coming back with the tea when she was accosted by Mabel.

'So, did you read my card?' she asked Rose.

'I suppose you mean the one which said :"Bill H is home makes a fine sailor oh he has grown have not seen him to speak to yet etcetera?".'

Mabel turned a rather reddish colour and her eyes nearly popped at the idea that others might have heard.

In another corner of the room, Ada and Louisa had found themselves in conversation about the drinks and spread for the reception. Ada and William had provided the drinks, glasses and trestles from the pub. Louisa was glad to able to sit down and talk.

'You know, when Ollie moves out with Tom, then only Mabel and Bill will be left at home, so I am hoping maybe we could leave the flat for a little house. I'd be near Fred in Kilmore. He's settled in there now.'

Ada said that she and William would not be going far, having the lodgings above the pub.

'But you know,' she continued, 'he's had the house built on the Wincaster Road for his mum and dad and they've not long moved in. Do you know what he's called it?'

'No, tell me.'

'St Anne's.'

'Why on earth?'

'France . . . he was born there, in Cannes, and lived there till he was ten or eleven. The chateau where his dad first worked was called Saint Anne's. Childhood memories, you know, for him and fond memories for his mum and dad. He's even had a plaque put on the wall and a brick with his initials. It's only small but there's a large plot at the back.'

Louisa wondered if her childhood memories would entice her to name any future abode.

'Does he speak French, then?' she inquired.

'At any opportunity he leaps at it,' replied Ada. 'If he had his way, we'd be living there now.'

Chapter 27

The post had become Gertrude's conduit for her own self-respect and love for her baby boy in the Haven of Hope. Every little message sent or received led her to believe in the relationship and kept alive her hopes that one day she may be able to hold him in her arms. The money she earned was dispatched to pay for his upkeep and she solidly refused the option of adoption in her correspondence with Miss Hurd. It would throw up a wall of silence and reject any maternal scrutiny. There would be a change of her son's name: the loss therefore of her dutiful-cum-legal relationship between her and Freddie.

What Gertrude didn't know but may have surmised was the fact that the Mission was operating in all illegality.

Adoption was illegal.

The mother could claim her child at any stage of the settlement between a family and the Mission even if she had actually settled for adoption.

The majority of the couples, sometimes of affluent and well-educated stock, could not conceive children and the Mission could help them by supplying them with a baby son or daughter. The child was then often disguised as an orphaned niece or nephew to avoid scrutiny. In so doing, it was of the utmost importance that the mothers should be held at arm's length by Miss Hurd whose blue printed paper contracts, although formal enough, had no legal basis whatsoever; nothing more than unfounded legalese on paper.

Gertrude and Olive spoke a great deal about the idea of adoption and its benefit, or lack of benefit, for baby Freddie.

* * *

One evening Gertrude came into the town to celebrate her mother's birthday. It was September and early evening. The summer was still very warm. August had seen a remarkable heatwave. As Gertrude walked towards Dog Alley, Ada emerged from the Square Brewery. With all the doors and windows open she had seen Gertrude coming towards the pub and felt it would be of interest to say 'hello'.

She disingenuously almost bumped into her as Gertrude's slight frame rounded the corner.

'Gertrude, what a surprise! We haven't spoken to each other for ages. How are you? I hear you've been back down the Borough for a couple of years now.'

Gertrude had been lost in thought and was totally unprepared for a meeting with Ada.

'Oh hello, Ada. Yes, it's nice to see you, too.'

'The last time we spoke must have been before you left.'

'Didn't we see each other at Olive's wedding?' Gertrude replied, as her brain stumbled through her options. She had avoided Ada for a long time and had no inclination to be reminded of her secret.

'Oh, yes that's right. But I don't think we actually had an opportunity to talk.'

'Yes, you're probably right. I came back more than two years ago from Claydon.'

Maybe that was too much information.

'How was Claydon?' asked Ada, who hadn't forgotten her original quest.

'Big and bustling but with nice parks and green areas.'

'Were the family nice?'

'Yes, they were thoughtful and considerate, and we worked hard, but I wouldn't want to go back.'

'Really?'

'No. Not really. It was too big. I rather prefer the size of the Lewis's boarding house and its guests.'

William put his head around the corner, said 'hello' to Gertrude and needing someone to serve, called Ada in.

Gertrude breathed a sigh of relief and headed to her mother's.

When Gertrude entered, she found Louisa amidst her five children. Rose had managed to find time and had come down on the train. Olive and Fred had brought *Aster and Morning Glory*. Mabel had made a dark blue shawl for Louisa. Bill, only in his mid-teens, gave his mother a brooch for her shawl. Gertrude gave her mother a small locket.

'Something for your secrets and happy birthday Mum!' Gertrude said to Louisa.

'Thank you, treasure.'

Gertrude looked around the room at her family and her former family dwelling. She noticed that the photos were back above the fireplace and asked her mother when she was going to find a mirror to place there.

'You know, sweetheart, that's the last of my worries. Anyway, as I get older, I don't really want to watch the continuous effects of aging. For the moment I've put the photos back, but in frames this time. It's just as well. They were showing signs of age. Fred did them for me.'

The passage of time had already wrought its havoc on Louisa, although she had been her own major stakeholder in her demise, especially with her marriage to an unreliable man, who had drunk himself out of the family and into a workhouse. Furthermore, Gertrude's hapless relationship had also reinforced the misfortune the family seemed destined to bear.

Mabel touched Gertrude's shoulder.

'We never really had time to talk at Olive's wedding, Gertie,' said Mabel. 'You know I may have found a man.'

'Mabel . . . are you serious?'

'As much as ever,' she said with a sparkle. 'What about you? What ever happened to Charlie? When you disappeared to London and he was sent to Ireland, did that mean the end?'

Gertrude thought it was all too much.

First Ada and now Mabel.

'Yes, it wasn't easy after he went, and I didn't want to be just a part-time girlfriend for a roving soldier.'

'That's a bit strong. I thought you two were serious?'

'Well, I was . . . and then the people in Claydon opened my eyes to one or two things.'

'About Charlie?'

'About men in general.'

'That's rather different to what you used to say before. You know?'

'I know. I think my experience with Charlie taught me a lot and . . .'

'Didn't you really love him, then?'

'Yes, I did, but I don't think he really loved me.'

Mabel looked at Gertrude questioningly.

'Yes, Mabel. I think it's a fact.'

'How can you be so sure?'

'One day I will explain,' she said, shrugging her shoulders and smiling wanly at her younger sister.

Rose interrupted them. The family wished Louisa a very happy birthday and she blew out the candles. Gertrude hoped her secret would remain as such, but Mabel had already noticed the change in her sister's demeanour: the absence of spring in her step and a saddened, if not unusually serious tone.

* * *

Gertrude returned to the boarding house feeling that the family had come together once more for the right reasons. Her brothers and younger sisters still had little inkling of what she had been through two years ago. How she wished that the family could have come together for her own bundle of joy. Since her stay at the Mission she had received regular news from Miss Hurd but, as she had told her mother and Olive, it seemed contrived and akin to a standard form of answer for any birth mother from the Mission.

The September heat had died down and the evening was drawing in. A lone blackbird sang in the trees in the lane and peace had settled on the fields where the herd of cows stood waving tails, munching and waiting to be led back into the byres.

That morning Gertrude had found herself in conversation with the postman, Frank. He pleased her. She knew little about him, but she found him tall, polite, and elegant. His eyes were honest.

Surrey

Chapter 28

Freddie, the suckling baby with short wiry hair reminiscent of his mother's own, had left her arms without knowing it and then been rocked and carried to and fro by nurses and different staff at the mission whose scents and voices were not like the one he had somehow known. His little frame filled out day by day until he was a bonny lad and clearly keen on surveying his surroundings at the age of six months. But now those nursery rooms at the Mission that Gertrude imagined her baby to be waking up to, filled with other cots and toddlers, had a become smaller and very different environment.

The front room of a small house in Guildford, some twenty-five miles from Gertrude's dwelling, had taken over.

Annie, the first child nurse to take in Freddie, was an elderly laundress.

She lived with her son and daughter-in-law who had already adopted a baby girl before their own child was born. As a result, fortuitously, both had grown up as close as brother and sister. Then Annie's husband had died, leaving her in a precarious situation. By taking in a child she could hope for a little financial relief, so she presented herself at the Mission and asked if she might become a child nurse to one infant.

Gertrude would never know that Freddie had virtually entered her own geographical sphere. It would be the nearest he ever came to her since his birth.

* * *

The house sat on a spur above the river and Annie often took him down to the ferry in the better months of his first year. He learnt to walk in her garden and his first words fell upon her. Her work as laundress was hard and she was no longer of an age to appreciate the physical labour involved. She had grown fond of Freddie, but as she moved into the second year of her charge, the Mission's payment to Annie had slowed. She was frustrated but did not know that Gertrude had paid two and a half years of keep and may have hit difficulties making both ends meet. The mystery of ever-later payments remained in the hands of the Mission.

In February she finally took it upon herself to claim the missing back pay and Freddie suddenly found himself in a tug of war between the two. The Mission had failed to honor the child's upkeep in time once again. As a result, one day Annie closed her front door in the Terrace above the Wey and pushed Freddie to the railway station where they caught the train to Waterloo, changed at Clapham and soon found themselves on Mrs. Willis's doorstep.

By April Freddie had moved north to Wood Green.

His second post-natal separation would leave him in the care of a woman standing on *Hirst House's* doorstep who spoke with a German accent, as it sounded to Miss Hurd.

She welcomed her in and took her to the office where she and Mrs. Willis were at work.

'Mrs. Müller, won't you please take a seat?'

'Thank you. I have travelled in the hope of seeing the little boy you wrote to me about.'

'Yes, I am sure you will see him later but first we must ascertain if you are suitably able to take him in,' replied Miss Hurd. 'Can I take some details, please?'

Mrs. Müller proceeded to tell Miss Hurd and Mrs. Willis about her past.

Now a fifty-year-old widow, Emma Müller had come to England as a child with her family in a wave of *émigrés.* Encouraged by talk of an improved life in North or South America, they sought a better and different existence to the hardships of failed crops in rural Hanover. Nevertheless, the first stage of the journey meant a stop in London where the parents conceded they could settle for the time being. Then the temporary arrangement became permanent, Emma met a young German baker-to-be and started a family. They had had four children of which three were girls. The older girl, Doris, was at home and helped. Dolly was at school and Nina a blouse maker; William was in a clerk's job in the export business.

The idea of a large family looking to take in a nurse child seemed to please Mrs. Willis. Furthermore, the fact that Doris would be at home suggested that the family may even be able to deal with two. She mentioned the idea to Emma Müller.

'That might be good for them both,' said Mrs. Willis. 'You see Freddie has been brought back here for financial reasons and we would like him to find a new happy home. First you must see the children and we will then come and see your home. The two would occupy you fully, of course, and I assure you we would cover their costs on a monthly basis. I assume that the family all speak English.'

'Yes, my children have all been born and brought up here.'

Mrs. Willis led her guest through the door into the large children's nursery decorated with high wainscoting, an unusual picture of a bear chasing a Japanese girl, and Freddie Carroll characters. A group of twelve children and two nurses were in the midst of tea. She pointed to two. The nurses looked up and ceased to help the children. The children in turn looked up. All were between eighteen months and three years old. They sat at low tables with tin mugs. They surveyed the visitor maybe intuitively knowing that somebody had come for them. As a group they seemed happy enough to Emma Müller, and she wondered why and how she should come here and turn this moment of relative tranquillity into chaos for this group of innocent faces. Two boys sat next to each other, one with brushed brown hair, dark eyebrows and a scowl and the other apparently content to rock on the legs of his little wooden chair.

Emma Müller felt the tension in the two children and crouched beside them. She held their little hands, said 'hello' and asked them their names. They remained silent, turned their heads and buried their faces in their tin cups.

Mrs. Willis asked the two boys if they would like this lady to be their mummy. The others watched the scene and moved their little heads.

They looked at Emma Müller again and one nodded.

'You must come back, Mrs. Müller, after I have been to see your home and then we will allow you to spend a little time with the children before departing with them. They both need a stable environment before they reach school age. Freddie has already had a child nurse and come back, and now he has attached himself to Frank. It might be better if they were to remain together.'

Mrs. Müller nodded and the two women left the room.

As she travelled back later that afternoon, she couldn't help thinking about the array of little faces seated and staring at her as she had come through the door to the nursery. She wondered what their looks were saying to her.

Maydurham

Chapter 29

1911

Gertrude had watched her sister's pregnancy with a sympathetic eye. Olive may have been indebted to her younger errant sister for the solemn reminder of what befell the unmarried single 'birth-mothers', the name given to them by the Mission. She would definitely not head down the same desolate road.

Life was like that: those who strayed were singled out quickly with deft family strategies and the prompt smothering of news abroad so that they could be moved safely out of sight and out of mind. Reputation was everything. Children were neither to be seen, nor to be heard in these cases.

Olive and Tom had married with a respectable number of months to spare.

Olive would have the baby at home in the family flat.

They had chosen Eric as his name: 'ever the ruler', according to etymologists.

Olive went into labour on the fourth day of October. The sky was overcast and grey and nothing but cold found its way up and down the High Street where pedestrians stood and conversed in overcoats and scarves. It had grown to be like this since mid-July.

The newspapers had been harking on about the prolonged spell of depressed temperatures. It may have resulted from the eruption of a volcano in Alaska in June leading to a significant decrease in the intensity of solar radiation, which, they said, may have been even greater than that for Krakatoa in 1883.

Louisa had stoked up the fire and tried her utmost to seal the windows and doors.

The baby arrived after the agonies and ordeal of a complicated night. Louisa and the midwife attended Olive and the child emerged but seemed to be lacking in activity. His cries were muted, and he appeared to be struggling to breathe. The midwife cleared his mouth and nose and gave him to Olive. She clasped him and thought about the days ahead and the plans she and Tom would now be making for another life in their midst. As Tom was constantly away, their address was here for the moment. New accommodation would be needed soon.

She tried to suckle the baby, but his nose ran, and he turned his head. He was trying to find his breath. He couldn't suckle and breathe simultaneously. It was either one or the other. He lapsed into a sleep drowsing with catarrh endlessly blocking his nose preventing him from finding a stable foothold in his new existence. The midwife judged that Dr. Panckridge should be called.

Overnight the condition worsened and the doctor, the midwife, Olive, Louisa and now Gertrude stood by the cot as the frail little figure tried to expectorate or breathe, to swallow or sneeze but nothing came of it. His temperature rose. He wouldn't feed and started nodding in attempts to find a rhythm or a breathing pattern, which would never come. His temperature rose again, and he still could not suckle.

By the morning of his second day the child was exhausted and diagnosed with pneumonia. Gradually the gurgling in his chest grew to its completion and he closed his eyes that had hardly ever opened, for the last time. The doctor uttered sympathetic words to Olive and pronounced the child dead. The undertaker was called.

The three women were left to their grief until Louisa summoned up the courage to call at the registrar's.

Gertrude stayed with Olive and in the quiet of the darkened room wondered how, of the six children Louisa had brought up, only Fred had managed to start a family. Mabel and Bill were younger, but the sisters seemed to carry a curse. Surely Rose with her Lupus disease and frail disposition would be left a spinster and childless, too.

This loss would be another sharp fragment of life's hard lesson plunged into the family's quest for peace, happiness and survival.

Olive was struck dumb and couldn't be consoled. There were to be no plans for a new family. Tom was on *HMS Indefatigable* and didn't know.

* * *

Eric was buried in a tiny grave near the railway line. The parents stood and watched as the vicar read and blessed the infant and then they retreated to the grassy bank behind them. There they watched from a distance as another steamer made its way up the line and reminded Tom that his compassionate leave was due to end shortly. A few minutes later the small group slowly made its way along the road passing under the Sussex Railway bridge and found itself back in the family's rooms. Nathalie joined them and the Campbell sisters gave the family their assurances for Olive's job and her welfare.

Chapter 30

One day in July, some eight months later, Louisa and Olive stood expectantly in Dog Alley as the sound of marchers reached them. They stood in the shade and peered down the street. The marchers turned the corner and made their approach to the square.

Neither Louisa nor Olive were particularly excited, but the curiosity of the Great Suffrage Pilgrimage brought people into town. After all, recent events had brought the country to the realisation that women's lives had to change.

These were Suffragists, and not Suffragettes whose direct action and controversial stances had leaked into the two movements and confused issues begging the questions whether one could actually do without the other, or whether militancy was the only answer to an unsuccessful albeit lawful movement. Millicent Fawcett and Emmeline Pankhurst, representing each movement, provided a debate that occupied Louisa's four daughters.

As Louisa and Olive looked down the High Street, it was clear that the women in long white, red, and green dresses with green, white, and red sashes, and ribboned bonnets, were supported by the locals. Some were on foot and some were wheeling bicycles. Townsfolk, too, wheeled bicycles. Young school children were present. The boys, dressed in long stockings and caps, looked on or accompanied the march. The girls stood with their mothers. The high

'Non-Militant' banner caused the gas lamp to sway on its wire.

'It's about time this country changed,' said Olive. 'And good luck to them. They've still got to get to Hyde Park.'

Louisa shrugged. They followed the stragglers to the Square where the leading representatives would speak and encourage the local women to join their movement and 'get the vote'.

A young and vibrant lady stood before the crowd and began a short speech:

'Ladies and also gentlemen – We embarked on this long pilgrimage from the four corners of this country to improve the future of women. Not the future for men, because they already have that in their hands, but they are nevertheless welcome to support us. As our leader, Mrs. Fawcett has already said: 'However benevolent men may be in their intentions, they cannot know what women want and what suits the necessities of women's lives as well as women know these things themselves, but what draws men and women together is stronger than the brutality and tyranny which drive them apart.'

Several people in the square stirred. Were they used to this?

Olive turned to her mother.

'Of course, she's right!' she muttered.

The young and vibrant lady continued:

'Of course, we women all want a certain equality and greater respect from our male counterparts and we are determined in our movement to reach our ends by non-militant and peaceful means; setting fire to houses, churches and litter boxes, as well as destroying valuable pictures never really helps to convince people that women ought to be enfranchised. We hate violence, and we are opposed to all violence, but we believe that women should have a share in the country. We pay taxes and should have some say in the making of the laws and in the spending of the money we contribute. There are already more than twenty marchers from the Maydurham branch. Please join, too, or support our movement in any way you can. You can donate or spread the word about our honest intentions to create a new world for women. You can even provide nourishment and drink for our marchers. Thank you to the people of Maydurham.'

Louisa looked at Olive.

'Right? Let's hope she is,' she retorted.

There was a round of applause and the speaker was helped down from the small stage erected by the statue for the occasion. Gradually the onlookers drifted away, some taking marchers to their homes where they found accommodation before the next day's trek.

The town seemed to have been invited to reflect on matters, which, although already latent in many minds now came to the surface.

* * *

Three months after the event, Rose appeared on Louisa's doorstep saying she had been to see her doctor. She was only twenty-three, but the disease had seemed to pinch her nose and flatten her cheekbones. Her mother wondered how Rose coped when she heard how her nasal passages seemed to constrict her breathing and affect her speech.

'Come upstairs, Rose.'

'You know, mother, Mrs. Tyndale gave me time off to come to see my doctor and to spend a little with you. Her husband's in Italy and she's going away for one or two days.'

'So, what did Dr Witty say?'

'That I am on quinine for the rest of my life and the bouts of fatigue and fever can occur anytime. Anyway, I already knew that. Did you hear about the McKenna fire?'

'The one in Stokeshott? Fred said something about it, I think.'

'Yes, did you know that the suffragettes burnt the house down?'

'No.'

'Well, apparently two of them made their way into the grounds . . . they'd driven from London and people had seen two women driving around the area . . . so they broke in and set the house alight with a paraffin lamp. Then they left a message from the *Votes for Women* people protesting against what they call 'forcible feeding'. They said the house burnt for over three hours, but nobody was living in it.'

'Forcible feeding? What do you mean?' asked Louisa.

'Well, you know, some of the women who get arrested decide to go on a hunger strike so that the authorities have to release them. The next thing, they find themselves being forcibly fed. Honestly I don't know why the suffragettes, when they get committed to prison for their actions, and apparently especially to Holloway, shouldn't refuse food, go on hunger strike and that way get released back into society . . . it's just their way of getting back at McKenna who's trying to make sure they are fed.'

Louisa looked at Rose and wondered about the tone of her daughter's voice which seemed to denote enthusiasm, and the look on her daughter's face which bordered on admiration.

'You're not getting radical by any chance, Rosie? Bit of a coincidence that Gertrude was in Claydon a few miles from Epsom when Emily Davison was knocked down and now you are few miles down the road from this. More and more young women are changing, burning post boxes, smashing windows and disrupting other people's lives. I'm sure I don't know what to think. And now the Tilly's portray women as angelic little demons. The world's gone mad!'

'That's the problem, Mum. You just said it. We are not supposed to think and see it as your generation sees it, and, I agree, the world *has* gone mad for the likes of those who don't want progress. You remember what Mrs. Badley said when she came to speak at the school? She said both constitutional and militant action was necessary, if we were to get the vote. And you heard that there were more than three hundred there to listen to her. Somewhere along the line there must be an ounce of truth.'

'Well, there's a rent to be paid and making a living to keep the body and soul together, and that's what we do. We don't have any men to look after our needs, and when we do, they aren't much use or are off in the services. The suffragettes are all well and good but I'm my own suffragette, I don't need them. Radical! As for the vote . . . well, seeing as the town's welfare depends on certain established families round here, I'd be surprised to see people vote them out.'

At the best of times Louisa was straight faced and found it difficult to muster a smile, but Rose thought she caught a glimpse of an ironic smirk on her mother's countenance. Politics seemed to trigger something in her.

Olive opened the front door and caught the tail end of the exchange.

'I suppose Rose has been telling you about the fire. I only thought yesterday that it couldn't be too far from her work. Good thing you don't drive, Rose,' she said with a laugh. 'Anyway, how are you, it's good to see you?'

'Well, I haven't had any of my dizzy spells lately so that's fine. And Mr. Tyndale is working on something that might interest William Lyndsey at the pub. He's painting in the Riviera and I have seen some of his work . . . it's beautiful.'

* * *

Another few months later Louisa and her youngest daughter, Mabel, stood under umbrellas and watched the Suffragettes march through town again in the cold pouring rain. It was early 1914 and hard to realize that these same marchers would soon be petitioning unsuccessfully for peace in the face of blind national interests.

PART 4

The Fourth Age of Man

Maydurham

Chapter 31

HOW LONG, O LORD?

How long O Lord, how long, before the flood
Of crimson-welling carnage shall abate?
From sodden plains in West and East the blood
Of kindly men streams up in mists of hate,
Polluting Thy clean air: and nations great
In reputation of the arts that bind
The world with hopes of Heaven, sink to the state
Of brute barbarianism whose ferocious mind
Gloats o'er the bloody havoc of their kind,
Not knowing love or mercy. Lord, how long
Shall Satan in high places lead the blind
To battle for the passions of the strong.
Oh, touch Thy children's hearts, that they may know
Hate their most hateful, pride their deadliest foe.

—Robert Palmer, 1888-1916
Hampshire Regiment

The postman came and disappeared. Sometimes Gertrude caught him and other times she wasn't sure if she really wanted to. Frank was tall, slim, wore a moustache, short light brown hair, a long straight nose and he carried himself bolt upright. Gertrude found him handsome and attentive and felt he had almost an equine look when he looked down past his long nose towards her as she took the post. Their families knew of each other. Her brother, Fred, had also recently joined the Post Office and ran into Frank every day at the sorting office before they set out on their rounds.

As Frank's fleeting father had disappeared, he grew up with his mother, Harriet Jane, and grandmother, Harriet, and at the age of eleven when his mother re-married and moved out, remained with his grandmother away from his mother's new family. Nobody was really sure who his father had been. His mother, Harriet Jane, knew but was not given to explanations.

They lived on the other side of the railway line behind the coal yards and the laundry. His grandmother was a laundress and took in clothes. Frank's dwelling was a five-minute walk, if that, from Gertrude's boarding house. The short narrow roads of rows of small red-brick houses were the more modest quarters to the west of the town in Frenchman's, both a portentous and coincidental moniker in Frank's case.

The two became more familiar and Frank was inclined to linger with the post in the hope of seeing Gertrude rather than the housekeeper. One blustery autumn morning he handed her some post and she told him she may be moving. He put his bicycle against the gate.

'Out of the area?' he questioned her.

'No, not really, were you worried?'

He smiled and with a wink said he wouldn't have thought about it.

'Mother wants to move out of the middle of town, and we might rent a small house. That's what she's always wanted. As she says, 'somewhere where she can put her feet up in the garden'. I think it will do us all some good. You know, the flat holds so many bad memories now. Maybe it's a way of turning over a new leaf.'

'Bad memories?'

'Yes, Olive's baby, stepdad's drunken fits, too. It all happened there!'

'Perhaps, it makes sense.'

A steam train puffed by across the fields, heading for Portsmouth Harbour station.

'Look, I can't stay here talking. I must get on.'

'Me, too.'

Frank left her and she carried the post inside. Among the different items there was a letter of receipt for her from the Mission for the money she had sent for young Freddie. With it she found a short message informing her that a lady from Chelsea had offered to become Freddie's guardian, which would help cover the cost of his upkeep and reduce the burden on Gertrude. Gertrude was more than grateful, but, nevertheless, felt she must continue to contribute to her son's welfare and wrote back saying so. Unknown to Gertrude, the *lady* was a writer and confirmed suffragette who contributed regularly to the *Votes for Women* newspaper. Parallel worlds of varying fortunes, coincidence and intervening persons bore the new century forwards.

Gertrude's pain had never subsided, but the tenuous connection with those she knew at the Mission and her meager contribution provided her with the hope that one day Freddie would be a young apprentice learning a trade and their paths could cross. As long as the Mission survived and Freddie was not adopted, a haphazard route leading the mother to the son still existed.

Her secret had never escaped, but if she should become involved with Frank, she was not sure if, or how much, she would be able to tell him. The risk of alienating him by admitting her own past of wantonness and irresponsibility and the relationship with Charlie seemed undesirable and might cast a shadow on their mutual understanding. It would also prevent her from feeling she was starting out afresh in a legitimate courtship. Frank was a permanent town fixture and not a roving soldier. Gertrude's traumatic past in Claydon could not be repeated.

A quandary persisted, however: how would she explain the payments from her own wages to a mysterious benefactor and any trips to Claydon, if they were required? And the moments when she found herself wiping the tears from her eyes for no apparent reason: how would she explain them?

Freddie was going on four-and-a-half years old and she thought about him every day. She imagined his growing features based on the now scanty and waning memories of his looks at birth and their desperately short time together; days that she had counted by the minute until Laura took him from her for the last time.

Now a new turn in her life beckoned with, maybe, the chance of founding a family, but her scar and its hurt still led her to long moments lost in thought and gazing into the distance when in the company of others.

One afternoon Olive and Gertrude found the time to take a train to Southsea to meet Lily. They congregated on the pier and gazed at the island across the water. The tide was out, and a fresh breeze played about the clear sky. The seagulls had formed a huddled group on the damp pebbles below them, seemingly imitating the groups of viewers on the pier. The three women pulled on their cloche bonnets to keep them firm.

'Got yourself a new young man?' asked Lily.

'I am not sure yet,' said Gertrude.

'He's fairly good looking but I think he's had an unfortunate upbringing,' added Olive. 'Mum's parents knew of the family for quite a while and he still lives with his grandmother in the Reeds. His mother left him with her mum when he was eight or nine to go and marry. None of them can write.'

'Frank can,' said Gertrude, a little defensively. 'He has to. He's a postman and he has to leave messages at some houses.'

'What about his father?' asked Lily.

'A bit of a mystery,' said Olive. 'His grandfather was a porter at the railway station and died before Frank was born, before our time. It seems that Frank may have been Harriet Jane's accident. When she moved out nobody knew who the man was. Except her, of course.'

'At least he was born and grew up in his own home,' said Gertrude, thinking that accounts of fallen women just seemed to enjoy only one outcome and wished that Louisa had been able to take care of her Freddie as Frank's grandmother had done with Frank. Despite their humble origins she knew that the upbringing of her family was different to that of children from Frank's area. Gertrude's family had sent her away; they had found the means.

Frank had preceded her by two years at the junior school and he told her that he had spent most mornings avoiding the rough youngsters coming into school from his part of town. His precarious background was nevertheless endowed by an air of gentility. Perhaps, he had been impressed by the frequent stories told of the polite airs his grandfather had displayed when working at the railway station collecting and pushing trunks and packages for the local landed gentry.

'Talking of family . . . Mother's had post this week from the Workhouse in the New Forest. They told her that step-father had died and asked if she wished to collect his belongings.'

'Will she, do you think?'

'I doubt it. He's been gone fourteen years. I don't know what he could have had of interest to mum,' Olive said.

'I thought you said he was in Droxford?' asked Lily

'Yes, he was, but maybe he was making his own way back home going west,' Gertrude speculated.

'Well, he's found it now, hasn't he?' Olive added.

Both young women looked out at the sea and felt the fresh breeze on their faces. Olive and Gertrude said they would like to take a tea somewhere, so they moved along the pier to the café.

'Anyway, I'm glad you may have found yourself a man. It's nice,' Lily concluded, as they sat down behind the glass screen overlooking the railings.

* * *

Gertrude and Frank had experienced similar disappointments: loss of father figures, illegitimate births, and relative poverty. But both aimed for a better future where life rolled itself out into a straightforward happy family environment, something that Gertrude's extended family had found in part, but something that Frank had never really enjoyed. He bore the feeling of being cast off by his mother as a child of misfortune. Consequently, he had been brought up for the greater part of his existence by a courageous grandmother.

He had succeeded in obtaining a job in the Post Office and for nearly ten years had been regularly employed in all aspects of its functions.

Since Claydon, Gertrude had worked her way back into society avoiding scrutiny and questions and Frank appeared as the ideal antidote to rumour. Notwithstanding, as a postman, he would find himself in a very exposed position to prying townsfolk when on his rounds; the type of prey that Ada would willingly quiz in a seemingly innocent manner.

Ada's curiosity had yet to wane; she had not forgotten Gertrude's acquaintance with a soldier and her ensuing disappearance to Claydon for work in a boarding house.

William was now too busy with the profitability of the Brewery to spend time on vacuous speculation about Gertrude's past romances. He was aware, however, that her sister Mabel asked questions about the welfare of William Henry. This alone made him disinclined to rake through Gertrude's family history. Should Mabel with her good-natured looks and obvious happiness take a shine to William then it might clearly turn out to be a fine match. If there was war, then he hoped his son would survive to see that day.

Unfortunately, and almost inevitably, events beyond the

country's control were soon to turn family aspirations or misplaced curiosity into something altogether irrelevant as Europe found itself sleep-walking into war.

Chapter 32

That particular Tuesday in August, Gertrude received a postcard from her younger sister fixing plans to go down to Portsmouth together Thursday afternoon.

"Shall be pleased to meet you at the station Th. Sorry to hear about the C hope she will soon be better."

The sisters hadn't gone anywhere for the Monday Bank Holiday. Mabel's shop was half-day closed on Thursdays and she liked to use the afternoon. The week would be sunny according to the weather forecast in the newspaper.

Gertrude stood at the gate to the boarding house and gazed over the fields and the railway line towards the hangers. Thoughts crowded in on her. She had just taken the post from Frank who seemed quite perturbed. He had heard that the stables in the area were soon to have their horses sent to Petersfield for veterinary inspection, if war was declared. The farmers in the area and the draymen would all lose their workhorses.

'They're sending them off to war,' Frank had said with a sigh. 'They'll be there before the men!'

Gertrude didn't know what to say. She had lived through the Boer War, which seemed so far away because it happened when she was in her teens. Fred had kept the family updated by reading the newspapers to them. It had seemed quite complex. France was much nearer.

‘They say it will be over by Christmas, though,’ was Frank’s parting remark.

For many war would come as no surprise. Grey’s famous words yet to become public already seemed clear in the minds of all. “The lamps are going out all over Europe, and we shall not see them lit again in our lifetime.”

Over by Christmas? If only, she pondered.

The Germans were already on the move and it was merely a question of hours before Britain entered the war.

Horses stood or cantered in the fields beyond the railway line and under the hangers. Gertrude thought of their welfare as they were to be herded into pens, and then trucks, and transported down to Southampton docks. Many would be used to draw gun carriages and canteens.

So how were the farming community going to bring in the local harvests: the hops and grain? Motor vehicles would also be requisitioned.

As she returned indoors, Annie Lewis took the post from her and told her that several of the resident vicars would be leaving the boarding house as they had been named as chaplains to a number of regiments.

‘Don’t worry, Gertrude, we will still require your services. It looks like a number of military people will be requiring billets. They’re also talking about manoeuvres on the Heath and opening a recruitment centre in the High Street.’

‘Thank you, Miss Annie. I am not that worried for myself, but for Olive’s Tom. He’s already at sea.’

The two women parted, and Gertrude attended to her kitchen duties. The bread was to be baked and meals for the evening and tomorrow’s breakfast were planned. As she kneaded the doughs, a thought occurred to Gertrude and she turned to Lily Alice who had just entered.

'So, Lily, what will happen when all the transport is gone or cut in half and we need flour and eggs to do all this?'

'Shortages, Gertrude! Shortages and then the prices go up. Then people will be rushing into the local grocer's and buying up all they can to make sure they're all right.'

The same afternoon Gertrude wrote a card back to Mabel :

Dear sister, will be there at 3 o'clock. Love from Gertie.

When Gertrude awoke the next day, war had been declared on Germany. The banks were closed until Friday and the following day passengers were asked to suspend plans to travel to the continent.

When the two sisters arrived at the station, they came upon the board that read:

TRAFFIC BY PASSENGER TRAIN

NOTICE IS HEREBY GIVEN THAT IN CONSEQUENCE OF THE EUROPEAN WAR CRISIS THE REGULAR PASSENGER TRAIN AND BOAT SERVICES USUALLY RUN BY THE RAILWAY COMPANIES MAY BE CONSIDERABLY CURTAILED OR INTERRUPTED, AND THAT TRAFFIC CAN ONLY BE ACCEPTED AS IT CAN BE DEALT WITH AND THEN ONLY ON THE UNDERSTANDING THAT RESPONSIBILITY WILL NOT BE ACCEPTED FOR ANY DELAY, DAMAGE, OR LOSS WHICH MAY ARISE THROUGH ANY SUCH CURTAILMENT OR INTERRUPTION

EXECUTIVE COMMITTEE

Gertrude and Mabel retreated to the High Street and decided that a walk around the lake would have to suffice.

As they reached the boats by the water's edge, Gertrude hesitated and looked out across the lake while her younger sister engaged with the boatman. She had come here with Charlie all those years ago. Where would he be, if war were now coming to a head-on confrontation? She knew he had served in South Africa and his last news had come from Dublin. His child was now lost to him and her, and their lives had moved on and . . .

Mabel interrupted her thoughts.

'Do you want to take a boat, Gertie?'

'We never really move on, do we?' she muttered.

'Sorry, Gertie, what did you say?'

'All right, you row.'

* * *

In the meantime, the colossal convoys of troops continued. The station gates were perpetually closed for three weeks as the X-trains passed though day and night at frightening regularity. The Expeditionary corps, with nearly forty thousand horses, was on its way.

The railways had become strategic and paradoxically suffered from lack of staff. The number of civilian passenger trains dwindled as coaches and trucks were requisitioned for troops, mineral, munitions and artillery. Going to Southsea would now be a rarity for the sisters.

Battersea

Chapter 33

Constance Maud descended the steps outside her comfortable Chelsea home and turned towards the river. She was intending to go across it to find another kind of life and another kind of person.

She had spent her September morning working with other suffragettes in the formation and future functions of the *Women's Suffrage National Aid Corps*. Its help in the coming months would ultimately lead to relief for the poor and destitute victims of the war as well as support for the soldiers abroad on the battlefields in the form of winter clothing. Secretaries, interpreters, visitors, cooks, and factory workers would find occupations through the *Aid Corps*. Women that Constance Maud had met would soon be dealing with refugees from Belgium and women designated as 'aliens' because of their marriages to other than British citizens.

This afternoon her mission was of a lesser, but altogether just as important, nature. Miss Maud was committed and generous; she gave time to the Suffragettes and fulfilled a second role by helping financially poor, illegitimate and unwanted children placed with foster parents. She wanted them to enjoy a better future. It seemed self-evident to her that with their pasts being the result of a sad miscalculation by adults, their futures should promise more. She was now morally and economically bound to ensure the prospects of three infants.

She crossed the Walk and looked out from the bridge towards the Old Chelsea Church and Albert Bridge. The wind blew in from the west and she held her bonnet. Images of Whistler's *Old Battersea Bridge* came back to her as she crossed but she felt safer here than on his old rickety structure.

On the other side she nearly bumped into several men smoking pipes in doorways in their shirt-sleeves and caught snatches of coarse language. Then she turned into the small warren of houses and knocked on a front door, which was opened by a young woman. In her rather square face she bore a piercing look below a determined set of eyebrows. She was probably in her late twenties and by her side stood a pretty girl with long brown wavy hair and big dark eyes who seemed to see right through Miss Maud.

'Hello. Mrs. Watkins? I am Miss Maud.'

'Thank you for coming. I was expecting you. Miss Hurd told me.'

'Well, it's not far and it's a pleasant walk. I live on the other side of the bridge.'

'Ah yes, with all the famous people,' said Hannah Watkins. 'Not exactly the same here. Run inside, Rose, and keep an eye on the children.'

The little girl disappeared down the passageway and Hannah Watkins ushered in Miss Maud. She caught sight of three little pairs of eyes as they peered at her in the semi-darkness. The two women sat down in the front room looking out on to the immediate road and red-brick cottage flats on the other side. They were relatively new but had weathered badly.

'My husband worked in Chelsea. He was a fishmonger. Cale Street.'

Miss Maud thought about it and saw the area.

'He brought home some very nice catches.'

'You have a lovely looking daughter,' said Miss Maud. 'How old is she?'

'Coming nine soon.'

'What's her name?'

'Rose Hannah, that's after me, of course.'

'And the little ones, how does she get on with them?'

'Well, you know, like most little girls, she loves their company and does try to help them get fed, washed and dressed. She's protective.'

Miss Maud looked around the rather modest but homely front room and listened to the chatter coming from the back room. Rose was calling Freddie for tea.

'As you know, Mrs. Watkins, I have assumed the responsibility of guardian for Freddie, Betty, and Rose, and I would like to be kept informed on how they are growing up, so I will leave you my address and I would be very pleased if you could send me a letter on a fairly regular basis. I know the war has started and things may happen, but . . . well . . . please just keep me informed, if you wouldn't mind. I suppose I should go through the Mission, but I would also like to be in contact with you and the children directly.'

'For your information, we call your 'Rose', 'Daisy,' said Mrs. Watkins.

'I beg your pardon,' stuttered Miss Maud. 'Oh, I see. Yes, two Roses would make things complicated.'

Miss Maud thought that she was perhaps a little too business-like with Mrs. Watkins and realized that it was probably the toll of the continual workdays with the National Aid Corps which had affected her ways of dealing with people. Nevertheless, it was true, people and things just had to move forward in the right direction.

'May I see the children, do you think?'

'Of course, would you like to come with me?'

She was led along the passageway and entered a small backroom kitchen where she saw two girls and a boy sitting at a low wooden table with a biscuit and a cup of milk. The boy had short brown hair, dark eyes, full cheeks and a dimple above his chin. He seemed happy and contented with his surroundings. He was the only boy and probably realised it. The girl called 'Daisy', and not 'Rose', looked up at Miss Maud. Fred looked up, too. They were well dressed, simply and ordinarily.

The smallest of the two girls stood and did a pirouette and curtsey for Miss Maud. Everybody laughed and applauded.

'Well done, Betty! That was sweet of you,' said Hannah Watkins.

'So, *you* are a dancer?' said Miss Maud and the little girl nodded and slipped gracefully back into her chair.

'And *you* must be Freddie?'

The boy nodded and smiled half-heartedly. Miss Maud seemed a lot older than 'mum'.

'Poor little things,' said Mrs. Watkins as they returned to the front room. 'Betty's mother was a dancer and she bandaged her daughter's feet so she could maybe become one, too, and just ended up stunting her growth. The most upsetting thing is that she has a twin and they're separated now. Freddie's quieter and says so much just by looking at you that he doesn't really need to speak. He's bright.'

Miss Maud understood that Mrs. Watkins cared dearly for these children.

'So, Betty might require dance classes and we must see how Freddie's schooling will start next year.'

'Yes, that would be important for both of them. You know, Miss Maud, they're a relief to me in a way,' said Mrs. Watkins. 'My own little boy, William, died five years ago and my husband died two years ago . . . both were too young to go. Of course, I have Rose and Louise, but I have no income apart from the allowances for the children from the Mission. Freddie's already been with two child nurses according to Miss Hurd and I know he needs looking after. And he's good for me, too. He reminds me of William.'

When Miss Maud returned the way she had come, the blustery wind picked up, the sun hit the river, then hid behind the clouds. She leaned on the bridge and wondered how many more people would be working with broken families and despair as the war progressed.

Maydurham

Chapter 34

Gertrude's, Mabel's, and Olive's trips to Portsmouth were curtailed and the family found that life had somewhat changed. The town square now lent its ear and gave its pennies to the Flag Day sellers at the markets every Wednesday. Talks at the Maydurham Women's Suffrage Branch became more vehement and concluded that equality should be reached. It was merely a question of 'upbringing and convention' that had to change.

Almost symbolically, Castle House, which had decorated the Square for so long was pulled down. It came as a shock to many to conceive of the disappearance of such a noble building. Its high-rise chimney stacks, pointed roofs, attic windows, broad and varied frontage covered in ivy was seated behind iron railings mounted on a straw-coloured brick wall. The edifice lent a genteel tone to the centre of town. Rumour had it that Pepys and Charles II had spent time there. Now there was talk of a bank taking its place. The modern age had come.

William puffed out his cheeks at what he saw, but realised that his pub would probably be useful to clear the dust from the workmen's throats, and the iron railings would help the war effort. Ada cursed the dust and took the curtains down regularly to shake them. When Mabel passed all three stood on the corner and watched the men at work, 'How's the family?' asked William

'Mother's talking of moving, but I don't know where to,' said Mabel?' said Mabel.

'Out of town?' asked Ada.

'Nearby, I think. Jubilee Terrace. That way.'

Moving had been on the women's minds. Olive was married and likely to leave. Gertrude lived with the Lewis sisters and William and Mabel were still in the flat with mother.

Gertrude felt that she might move before any of them. Her relationship with Frank had begun to take form and, although it was only early days, they seemed happy in one another's company. Gertrude found that he was caring. He looked after his grandmother and helped her organise the laundry. That seemed to be his first priority. Nevertheless, if they should both marry and continue in employment, then in due course they may be able to find their own home.

The war tainted the local citizens' thought patterns; what was once sure and certain now appeared uncertain. Farmers lacked horses, hands and transport. Tradesmen found the same problems. The Post Office relied on bikes and longer rounds with the increase in work and fewer men. Frank was happy to oblige.

One day the couple walked down to the seat at the end of Gertrude's road and looked up at the South Downs running east to the Sussex coast.

Frank stroked his moustache then pushed his hands down on the seat in a signal of earnestness and turned to Gertrude.

'You know, Gertie, if ever I can be sure of surviving the war, then maybe we could start a family, get married.'

'Do you think you'll go?'

'Well, as I look after grandma and I'm employed by the Post Office, plus the fact that I don't want to volunteer, it looks that I could avoid the war as long as it doesn't last too long.'

'Are you saying we should wait for the war to finish?'

'No.'

'So why don't we marry without waiting for the war to finish anyway?'

'You're probably right. But I can't help wishing to marry in peacetime. You know when folks like us are a bit more inclined to celebrating something.'

'That may never come. Olive's naval friends have seen the awful scenes down at Portsmouth Harbour when they've brought back the wounded. They say they don't stop coming in. I am not sure we can wait to be happy, Frank.'

* * *

Within a year brother Fred had walked Gertrude down the aisle and she had finally married Frank. They moved into a terraced house between the Old Workhouse and the station. She was already bearing a child to be born six months later, her second baby. But this one was allowed and would be able to find his own niche in the family and friends that would surround him. They called him 'Harold' because of Frank's grandmother and 'Albert' because of the former Prince.

Nevertheless, moments of regret hit Gertrude when she was alone with her new baby and similar memories flooded back. She wished she was cradling both. The perplexity of Freddie's whereabouts and the constant burden, even today, of the maternal self-denial imposed by the stigma of illegitimacy, had worn a terrible path in her thoughts.

'*Charlie's off fighting a war somewhere and somebody's looking after Freddie, and I am looking after one child instead of two.*'

Images of two baby boys, half-brothers and cousins to other children in the family that might have been, ran through her mind. Hope of a chance encounter or a reunion with her estranged infant never died within her.

Jutland/Skagerrak

Chapter 35

1916

Time had gradually rolled itself out, bringing disappointment and struggle to the family, as well as the forces of antagonism and rivalry to the people of Europe. The navies spread mutterings of *Der Tag* within their midst and the cornerstone to British strategy was the prolific production and launch of Dreadnoughts designed with colossal firepower, improved armour, and greater speed. They were the means by which, for once and for all, the enemy would be prevented from challenging British naval supremacy and posing a threat to its empire. The enemy had tried to keep up and one piece of technology, their armour-piercing shells, stole a march on the British.

The governments and peoples mutually held each other in contempt and propaganda flooded the channels of communication.

German citizens in Britain were eyed with suspicion and internment and repatriation schemes found themselves underway. A feeling of preparation for war had prevailed ever since the flurry of treaties done and undone. The Austro-Hungarian, Greater Serbian, and Russian talks over the years had sown their seeds of instability and provided

Europe with its own powder keg. Britain and France watched. France needed Russia and vice-versa. Britain was unsure of its relationship with Germany. German strategy wavered but was fixed with the events in Sarajevo.

Then the German trains brought hordes of soldiers through Belgium and Great Britain could do nothing but declare war. Even the sisters' conversations brought up the consistent argument that two cousins were going to war, which sounded reprehensible and unfathomable. Mabel, the youngest, and Olive, the eldest, were at a complete loss. Wilhelm II, or Kaiser Bill, had been to Cowes and George V had gone to Wilhelm's daughter's wedding, British ships and navy officers had been at the 1914 Kiel Week together saluting the Kaiser. Both regal heads descended from Victoria whose funeral had also brought Wilhelm to England. Nothing seemed right to the four sisters.

Olive had hardly seen Tom since their marriage and the loss of Eric, but she knew his life and thousands of others were tied up in the ever-increasing race against the build-up of arms and fleets in Germany.

Tom had embarked on *HMS Indefatigable* nearly four years ago. Olive knew he was in Scotland somewhere; the men provided scant detail. Distance and duty left the men with little time with families and friends. They were lucky if they were able to see their families every fifteen or so months. Information was scarce and letters and post cards were the best many couples, or families, could manage. The women at home had become virtual war widows before their time. They spent time trying to remember the man they had once married. The men spent hours on drills and daily ship duties in expectation of *Der Tag*. Their lives were beyond family and beyond comprehension. The outlook was purely a vision of a sea battle to end all sea battles.

Just when war was declared *HMS Indefatigable* had missed an opportunity for a first encounter. Tom had been on board in the Mediterranean and in pursuit of the German ships that had pounded French positions in Algeria, but the German battlecruisers slipped away. The adrenaline of combat had seized the men only to be frustrated by orders not to pursue their prey.

Now Beatty's Battle Cruiser Fleet and Fifth Squadron were at berth in the Firth of Forth. The funnels smoked idly as crews went about their drills and duties. The clanking of metal, the sound of whistles, and the routines never seemed to end, but, unbeknown to all, the order to put to sea was imminent and so was the fateful day.

Tom had gone ashore at Queensferry to send a card and was making his way back with two other turret gunners when they stopped at the ferry pier and saw the 'steaming signal' hoisted on the ships. 'Raise steam for 22 knots and bank fires at half an hour's notice.' The men caught the boat to *HMS Indefatigable* and went aboard. For the next three hours, all of the complement was accounted for, the gangplanks and small boats raised, the searchlights and guns were uncovered, and as the time gradually ran down, the men went over the procedures of engagement time and again.

The May evening light grew weaker but kept a gloomy grey as the proud and mighty ships raised anchor and steered their passage out of the Forth under the bridge. Tom stood by his turret and wondered if it was to be the moment they had all prepared for. Smoke filled the air and left trails back into the city. The patriotic crowds on the hill watched as Beatty's low-lying fleet disappeared ghost-like into the North Sea and over the horizon.

The waters were calm and at daybreak in the cooler hours the crew completed their deck-washing duties, signals and drills and ate breakfast. Tom looked around as the Petty Officer entered the turret and checked its content and orderliness. The stern turret door stood open and caught the rising sun. The men seemed inquisitive and keen. They were approaching the north eastern waters or straits separating Denmark from Norway and Sweden. Some called the area 'Jutland', others 'Skagerrak'.

'All in order?' the officer asked.

'Sir. Yes, sir. Any news, sir?'

'Nothing for the moment, Hill.'

'Just another sweep, sir?' asked Beeston.

'We'll find out soon, no doubt, men.'

The Petty Officer checked the drinking tank, urinals and biscuits, first aid bandaging and corned beef and made his way back to midships. There were calls down the hoist shafts and their mechanics were checked.

Little did the fleet know that the Admiralty had erred in their message, which put Reinhard Scheer's High Seas Fleet still at berth in Wilhelmshaven. In fact, he had steamed out at 02:30. This miscalculation would lead to a surprise discovery for Beatty's ships some twelve hours later. This unfortunate sequence of events was compounded by the fact that the first ever maritime aerial reconnaissance had succeeded in locating the German fleet, but its information failed to reach Beatty's ship.

Thus, it transpired that, unbeknown to thousands, the

ferocious and sometimes ill-coordinated engagement was now minutes away. Furthermore, it was about to commence in strange circumstances: the German scouts stumbled on and investigated a Danish tramp vessel and in so doing were drawn into the view of the British.

Eighteen and a half hours of peaceful sailing from Queensferry now turned into the most violent sea battle ever recorded.

Tom's crewmen were called into action a few minutes before four o'clock in the afternoon. The bugle's call had gone some time ago and action stations were manned everywhere. The ship had followed the pack first on an eastward bearing and then a turn to the south running parallel to the enemy as the first blows to the ship's body were taken. The gunners opened up and pitched their shells at their designated target, the *Van der Tann*. The first salvoes fell beyond her and the men tried to correct with the help of the indicator before their eyes.

HMS Tiger, further up the line, lit up with several hits and lost control of two turrets. The deck was gradually packed with wounded and dying men hit by fragments of flying steel from pierced armor. The stretcher bearers picked up the dying and severely wounded and found no time to even reflect or come to terms with the inescapable shredding of human bodies and lives before them. This is what they had waited for and trained so long for.

Tom's turret in *Indefatigable* still sought to pound the *Van der Tann* using the director indicator. Everything was carried out according to the years of training. The colossal roar as the shells flew out deafened the gun-layers and drove vibrations through the whole turret structure. One shell left, another shell left, another again, but they hadn't even yet straddled the *Van der Tann*.

Then in a split second, before they could load another round, a colossal flash and tremor travelled through the ship's beam sending guns, funnels, turrets and men into the air like matchsticks. The three hundred tons of arms of a virtually fully laden *Dreadnought*, combined with fuel oil and coal, exploded, turning bulkheads into flying girder shrapnel and splitting the vessel in two. *HMS Indefatigable's* engagement had barely lasted five minutes.

The crews of *HMS New Zealand* and the *Van der Tann* looked on incredulous at the unspeakable spectacle.

The stern separated and sank below the still waters as the bows and midships struggled on and then sank some five hundred yards further. A thousand men had gone. The smoke, flames and masses of debris from the explosion had risen more than a hundred meters. When the yellow cloud cleared nothing remained.

* * *

Two days later Beatty's Battlecruiser Fleet limped back under the Forth Bridge early in the morning bearing their scars: scorched funnels, blistered paintwork, gaping holes, shattered or hanging masts. *HMS New Zealand* found her berth and the survivors stared at the buoys around which *HMS Indefatigable* had swung before moving off. The hospital ship moved in and the mutilated and burnt were given as much succour as could be provided.

The eight thousand seven hundred men lost from both

fleets left their indelible marks on the admiralties, the devastated families and the general public.

Britain wondered what had happened to its maritime invincibility. Germany wondered how it could sortie back out into the North Sea after its losses.

Paradoxically, the staggering numbers of men killed in the Somme were rolling off the press and dwarfed the dreadful figures from the North Sea.

Maydurham

Chapter 36

Tomorrow would be Saturday and Olive hoped that the sisters might be able to see a Wilkie Bard show at the King's Theatre. That would change their spirits.

She put on her pinafore and started picking up the newspapers left next to the armchair in the drawing room giving on to the garden. The usual advertisements plastered the front page: The Swan Fountain pen, Ficolax- The Fruit Laxative, You are safe with Boots Chemists, Models Statuettes and Memorial plate by the Goldsmiths and Silversmiths Company.

Agnes Campbell had departed the world in January and her sister Susan continued to employ Olive. She took her breakfast, helped Olive with the objects lying about the drawing room, finally readied herself and proceeded to the post office to buy stamps and send a parcel to a friend in London.

The queues in the proud Victorian building were unusually long. Susan progressed slowly and overheard concerned murmurs from certain people leaving the building about the telegrams received.

What appeared to be parents were moving towards the door.

'He says they docked this morning and he's safe.'

When Susan arrived at the glass-panelled counter she handed over her parcel and collected her stamps.

The middle-aged woman and her greying husband in the next queue collected a telegram. The woman's face turned pallid and she gripped his arm and, in what seemed to be an act of support, he edged her towards a bench near the entrance.

'Are you all right, Mrs. Parr?' enquired an acquaintance, standing in a queue near the couple. Then she turned to the woman's husband. 'Do you need help?'

'It's no matter,' said the man. The couple sat on bench before the doors.

'They said he'd gone missing and now this,' said his wife wiping her nose with a handkerchief. She waved the telegram in front of the other woman.

'Let's go home, sweetheart.'

The couple slipped out of the door and down the steps. Several bystanders in the post office turned to each other with compassionate looks. The times had brought terrible sadness and trauma to waiting families.

'Poor souls,' said the man behind the glass panel to Susan. 'There's messages coming in from Scotland this morning. Men safe. You know. Sounds like something big out at sea.'

Susan returned to the Avenue but proceeded beyond the house and stood at the end of the road overlooking the lake where she considered how she might even touch on the subject of what appeared to be the aftermath of a large naval engagement with Olive.

When she slipped discreetly back into her own house, she knew that her looks probably would betray her to the young thirty-two-year-old woman with auburn hair, whose classic and yet humble and confident demeanor would probably dissolve into incomprehension, misplaced hope and tears. How would she come to understand the words tripping from her employer's mouth?

She called to Olive who was changing a bed. When she came downstairs, Susan Campbell was standing by the fireplace. Turner's print was hanging behind her.

* * *

By the next afternoon the murmur had grown beyond gossip into the news of a terrifying full-scale naval disaster. Olive and Susan Campbell sat in the back room poring over the newspaper, which gave little indications other than the facts that 'six vessels which disappeared beneath the waters' had been manned in Portsmouth. That was more than indicative for Olive. The likelihood that Tom would be amongst those 'who will return no more' seemed high.

The newspaper was well-informed. Its accounts were out on the wires and in print. Its operators were continuously collecting briefings from the admiralty and the news grew starker by the minute. The latest editions rolled out.

'*HMS Indefatigable*' had been sunk.

Olive would never receive the 'docked and safe' telegram.

* * *

Sunday morning, William Lindsay was standing by the pub door thinking about the terrible losses of life in the Royal Navy when Gertrude passed by. She acknowledged him and he asked the inevitable question about Olive's husband and Gertrude looked forlorn.

'Please give her all our sympathy,' he mustered.

It was too easy. Thank God that William is in the Home Fleet.

Chapter 37

1917

'Shortly after their marriage, Frank, Gertrude and Harold had moved into a small terraced-house situated in a short cul de sac running parallel to the railway line. Looking over the bank at the back they sometimes watched the trains carrying troops and waved.

The day that Frank and Gertrude had dreaded had finally come.

* * *

Gertrude sat at the kitchen table; her abundant lively curls tumbled down the side of her still youthful face. The cat licked at the saucer and the smell of the tuna wafted about the kitchen. Harold ran up and down the narrow garden path. Barely three years old but communicative, full of energy, and gentle. So much yet to learn from a father in the time he still had, which would be all too short.

The front door opened, and footsteps moved up the corridor. Gertrude looked up at the clock over the stove and sighed. Time was no longer hers, and her husband's was gradually slipping away, too. Frank set his bag under the kitchen table and looked her in the eyes. Harold bounced in through the back door. Frank put him on his shoulders and stood, the boy beat his father's head and then pulled on his long moustache. Frank smiled all he could.

'Did you see grandmother? Would you like us to walk up to the station with you?' Gertrude asked.

'Yes, that would be the best,' replied Frank.

'Daddy, are you going away?' joined in Harold.

'Yes, but not for long, and when I come back, we'll all go down to the sea,' he replied, turning his face in all earnestness to Gertrude's. She looked, too, but saw nothing.

Still carrying the boy on his shoulders Frank stood in the little garden and looked at the short privet hedge, the gate and the bushes on the bank overlooking the railway line. They hadn't much but it was a start. His job as a postman had stabilized things and Gertrude had been able to work in the shop while her mother had kept Harold.

The rose bushes on the south-facing brick wall were blooming; a lasting sense of place and time hung in their fragrance and elegant form. Only glimpses could he now afford. His contemplation was elsewhere, embedded in the nagging sentiment of separation and fear. He turned and moved back into the little kitchen. Gertrude put on her hat and they descended the steps to the pavement.

Grim with foreboding, the three persons edged their way up the road towards the railway bridge, down the hill, passing between the Methodist and Catholic churches and then found themselves on the platform. Only the red and white signal and the closure of the crossing gates stood between them and goodbye. The plume of smoke could be seen before the train itself came into sight.

* * *

Gazing from the train window, Frank recorded the embankments, ponds, overhanging bushes and fields as they rushed by. Some he had wandered through as a boy, others he knew from hearsay, especially the spectacles of the racecourse and the motor racing circuit. The beckoning empty stand overlooking the white fences and thick grass had seen its last *Eclipse* winner *'Hapsburg'* nearly 3 years ago. The famous motor racing circuit would soon be used for other purposes. Moments of leisure had now taken on a different cloak at this fearful time. Smiles and laughter were rare.

His occupation as postman had devolved into that of an infantryman; a private. His postman's occupation was not starred, so there would be no waiver for his enlistment, although he had spent his time trying so hard to make many ends meet for those around him. His grandmother still survived taking in laundry and he continued to help her. She had brought him up. His heart was heavy and, in some way, bitter. He had understood the Cavell stamps on the letters he delivered and listened to the encouragements of the Derby man. But he knew he was of more use here. Nevertheless, his mind's eye had caught a glimpse of something else and he had enlisted. Was it the pressure of the community?

He had promised Gertrude and Harold they would take the train down to the coast when he returned.

* * *

Gertrude brought Harold home and sat with her three sisters in her front room overlooking the small cul-de-sac. This seemed to be a special occasion. They speculated on Frank's journey and, unconsciously, on his final destination.

Men seemed to be very expendable items and the newspapers numbered the dead and missing day by day by the thousand. The circuits of the British Empire had been worked and worked, bringing men back home wounded and taking others back out to patch up army units in the Middle East, the Mediterranean, and France.

The sisters paused. Harold got off Gertrude's knee, scampered back into the kitchen, and chased the cat out into the garden. He stood before the rose bush and remembered the look in his father's eye as he had beheld the precious flower on its long and slender stem. Something inside the plant had drawn his father to silence and brought on a distant gaze. He had sensed his father's thoughts straying and tugged at his father's chin to regain his attention. What moments were these? Their strangeness would haunt him for a long time; a strangeness that he would not understand, an awful stillness or emptiness that would dwell in the child.

The four women looked at each other and the natural silence impeded their desire to talk. A sigh. Another silence. Another strange and awful moment. Olive was sorely reminded of her own husband's departure. The parting on the same platform, as if history must inevitably repeat itself. All that was left to keep her company were the memories of their child that had not lived and the photo of the serviceman with a neat moustache.

"You know, Gert, when Tom set off, we all thought it would be just a question of time before he was back down from Scotland. He told me on the platform that confidence was sky high, the ships were unsinkable, and that Jellicoe and Beatty were very respected men. But one man, just one man responsible for so many. I suppose they must have known just what he was doing. But you saw the papers, didn't you?"

"Perhaps, in the army it's different," said Gertrude. "Maybe they can master situations better. At least, Frank's with Holly. They are good for each other."

Rose leaned back in her chair and thought about the fate of her two anguished sisters. She knew *she* would probably never meet a man; her ungracious and curious face had suffered from her continuing and terrible ordeal with Lupus.

Harold stood at his mother's knee. He tugged her skirt and she picked him up and the others watched.

The clock on the mantelpiece ticked on.

Gertrude's face clouded over. Thoughts of Charlie and Freddie emerged, still her secret. She decided to take Harold to the lake. Rose, ever attentive, said she would come. Mabel returned to her draper's shop. Olive accompanied them as far as the house in the Avenue.

As they descended the bank to the lake, Harold called for a boat ride and Gertrude obliged. The boatman pushed them off, Rose held Harold. Gertrude rowed, gazing into her little son's eyes, seeing more, feeling more than her heart could take. When there was one, she inevitably saw two.

Her secret had remained untold. All those years ago when she had disappeared for several months in service she had been shielded from virtually all, but she still wore a distant gaze on her young face. Occasionally, when her sisters had raised the subject with her, she used her unruly curls rolling down the side of her face to hide her looks.

The scar was still there some eight years later. Now

Frank had come into her life and brought her happiness and a child, but why had everything gone so wrong at the age of twenty? First Dublin and now France?

The water lapped at the bows of the little boat and she manoeuvred around the rushes and the shallows. There was peace here. Nature was at one here and knew its role. The swans, ducks and moorhens rocked on the gentle waves and passed their time much as the clouds come and go with no need to ponder. The afternoon sun drifted overhead, and Gertrude contemplated the little isle she was gradually approaching. Turning the boat, she pointed out the nests and birds to Harold. The two sisters played animal guessing games and Harold asked them if they could draw when they returned home. Now that she was alone with Harold, Gertrude vowed she would devote herself entirely to him.

For how long?

Why had this motherly devotion been refused before?

As they moved past the island, she thought that it reminded her of a painting she had seen; an oarsman guiding a small boat towards an island of cypress trees and craggy cliffs.

At the landing stage the boatman helped them out and they wandered round the lake to a convenient little spot where the ducks would eat the bread thrown at them. Harold's blonde curls lifted as the west wind blew across the water and brought the crumbs back to the shore. He waited for the ducks to congregate and threw the remains. Gertrude and Rose had found a bench and watched him.

'When's daddy coming home?'

'It may be a while.'

'Will he be as long as Uncle Tom?'

'I don't know, sweetheart.'

Gertrude turned her head and looked at the old barrow behind her, a Saxon burial tomb, now just one of numerous mounds with conifers and oak trees waiting for walkers and children to trample over them once again.

The brass band had played here weeks ago, during which time Gertrude and Frank had listened as Elgar's music wafted down the hill. The crowd in which they found themselves sang but didn't sing, Gertrude thought, and, similarly to most people present she felt the awful question in their minds. Why persist with such misplaced music? How many had now been lost in Flanders, the Middle East, the Dardanelles, the Somme and Jutland? But it wasn't just the music, it was the message and the promotion of the message and only one message: the forever-rallying cry for victory. It was as if the countries of Europe had their heads in a vice and couldn't think differently. The town had seen the Suffragettes march and heard the call for peace. All had gone unheeded, ignored, and only entrenched attitudes were to prevail.

She thought about Charlie again and wondered where he would be now.

The three figures rose from their bench and walked back through the town. As they crossed the square, William Halden, left his pub and came towards them past the statue in its centre.

'Has Frank gone?' he asked.

Gertrude looked beyond him and then at him and managed to say, 'Yes.'

Harold tugged at his mother's sleeve and Rose told William that Frank had taken the early afternoon train.

William watched as they crossed the square.

Flanders

Chapter 38

1917

Private Charles Soloman and his battalion had been through traumatic military reversals. Having returned to England from Gibraltar at the outbreak of war and then disembarked at Zeebrugge, the men had been overrun at Ypres where Soloman had escaped capture and survived. The Allies' retreat from the Belgium border had brought them much further south. The men had fought a long, slow and organized rearguard action and the enemy had been halted.

It was All Saints' Day and he stood outside the Saint Vaast Church with several other bandsmen and drummed his way through the memorial service to the fallen French and British. The size of the church dwarfed the small group of soldiers and bandsmen who had paraded to and from the *Grande Place*.

Soloman turned to his companion:

'Plenty of churches round here called Saint Vaast . . . must have been popular!'

'All the same to me, Sammy,' came the reply. 'I don't get involved in religion.'

Saint Vedast had risen some 1300 years ago in a luminous

cloud near Arras before leaving his teachings in place and a colossal array of buildings.

When the bandsman took off his cap and sidled into the church he was struck by the beauty of the edifice. The blackened redbrick structure over the large gothic door gave the lie to the outstanding pillars, vault, and stained-glass windows inside.

'Going into churches seems to make me think,' Soloman said when he came out and found Kerridge waiting. 'You know, here we are living on borrowed time, and when you walk into one of these places you feel so grateful to be a witness to a place of such beauty. I do hope I'll be able to come back and see it again one day.'

Charles Soloman's army life was built on skirmishes, bombardments, trench-building and relief work for other battalions in the sector. The horrors of Ypres and the anxiety of the retreat had given way to a regularity of patrol and sniping defence, responding to artillery fire and keeping the lines. The men had even taught the school children in the town how to use electric torches and gas masks, how to escape the enemy bombardments, and how to find safe shelters. The occasional football match punctuated a wary and tense phony rhythm to the war.

* * *

When the onslaught of Operation Michael finally came on the first day of spring 1918, the enemy trapped Soloman's battalion near Saint Quentin with their furious final drive.

The men crouched as the colossal barrage started at 4:30 in the morning. Gas shells and shrapnel fell around them.

Many had never heard anything as monstrous. The pounding ran north-south and then south-north for five long hours. When the guns fell silent, an overwhelming ground mist loomed and hid the advancing German divisions outnumbering and confounding any serious response from the redoubts.

In little time the soldiers were overrun and the group of men in Redoubt 50 found themselves in the hands of Germans. Soloman and others threw their hands above their heads and were pushed towards the enemy's rear lines. Their arms were collected and the machine guns which had fallen into enemy hands were checked and sent to the rear.

The soldiers were embarrassed, humiliated, and saddened and yet somehow sure that their fate might yet change with a counter-attack as the Germans hurried them from the field as quickly as possible; pushed on in the fog past narrow gauge trucks bringing up munitions, pushed on past the heavy artillery pieces covered in netting and hidden under dripping trees, pushed on past the last shards of a village and on to a supply road with the mist doing its best to linger about them. Pushed on and on over several miles until a field surrounded by barbed wire came into sight into which they were herded, and where it seemed they might be held for several days.

Soloman cast his eyes about the flattened muddy area and understood it was nothing more than transit. Nothing fixed or permanent seemed available, apart from tents and more tents. They were to line up in their ranks and in the remnants of their battalions after which the count and first basic identifications were made. More and more prisoners poured in until the evening, when their flow became a trickle of stragglers and armed guards. The wounded were treated with scant attention. The Germans had barely any medical supplies or bandages and they provided merely straw beds for those who suffered.

The following morning the able men were marched further back behind the lines to a railway halt and ordered to work unloading the trains and filling the trucks. Soloman's stomach churned on nothing. They had been given nothing other than stale loaves of bread, with the result that the energy of the weakest amongst them was sapped by the minute. He watched the guards push several men around trying to hurry them. Then they picked out a group and sent them back towards the lines.

The Germans shouted: 'Blessiertenträger! Blessiertenträger!' and gave signs with their hands. Soloman was also pushed forward and ordered to follow the posse. They picked up wounded soldiers and brought them back over the fields. They had never been this close to the enemy. They had never handled the enemy. They had never had to understand the enemy. The survivors from Soloman's battalion soon noticed the awful welfare of the German soldiers; young conscripts, poorly fed and likely to die from a lack of medical teams and supplies before they could even escape the front.

* * *

A week later, emaciated and hungry, Soloman found himself in the lines of prisoners detrained from trucks in Cassel. Their march took them past the sentries and into a compound of wooden huts with a range of low-lying mountains in the distance. They were away from the fighting, later to be cursed as POWs and cowards and unable to do anything about it.

Late spring, the men were moved to Hameln and finally reached Soltau in August. Unknown to them, since April they had been retreating ahead of the Allies' advance. Only scraps of news and rumours of the Allies' progress on the front circulated, and their truth was impossible to ascertain. Proper food rations were hard to come by and even the German guards were clearly undernourished. The only food, if available, was sausage with bread and root vegetables. The Germans working the fields around them paid the prisoners no heed.

Nevertheless, it was not the captivity that would finally affect the men the most, but the overall health conditions of the weakened and undernourished communities and the spread of illness. Russian soldiers were on the other side of the camp. They had been there longer. Like all, they were famished, but food parcels and post rarely came for them. The camp guards were the only contact with the outside world. They were also the conduit for the influenza epidemic.

Six months of detention in camps had elapsed. Summer was about to turn to autumn, cooler times, but at the same time, the prospect of damp. The men knew the camp had been built on reclaimed marshland. Each day they stood at the fence and looked at the heather, the gorse and the drain ditches. The failure of proper nutrition continued to sap their morale. Soloman contracted a cough that he couldn't shake off and the orderlies took him out of his hut to the infirmary. The German doctor examined him.

'Do you have contact with the guards?' came the question.

'What do you mean, please?' Soloman replied.

'Do you speak to the guards, take things from them . . . you know, relatively close contact.'

'I don't understand.'

'Do you have nausea or hurts? You know, pains?'

'Yes, I have pains in here,' Soloman pointed to his chest.

'Well, that is good news. It is not Spanish influenza.'

'You say you are tired, but everybody is tired. We all eat badly and now the autumn is coming.' The doctor remained prosaic.

Soloman returned to his hut. The men looked at him sheepishly hoping 'Sammy' would soon be able to play again for the English POW team.

That night he started a chill and sweated profusely. In the morning he coughed up blood and he was put into quarantine.

Chapter 39

1918

William Henry Halden was standing on the deck of HMS Monitor 26. Not a particularly tall man, but a broad and angular frame, appealingly natural and full of self-confidence and goodwill.

The anxiety and then the boredom of two postponements and two returns to their waiting station off Dunkirk had eaten into the crew's nerves. Waiting and waiting while Keyes and his officers deliberated, shut up in the small mess. Going through the routines or leaning on the Monitor's rail as the ship mirrored the listlessness of the other ships lying at anchor. Too much time to think.

Then, finally, a third order to sail came through and that mission ended in failure.

Now a few weeks later, William Henry looked north-east as the convoy moved out yet again. When they reached their designated area, it was midnight and the conditions were fair. The gun turrets were trying to find their bearings in the gentle pitch and roll whilst the smokescreen began to build. Sand was being shovelled on to the deck floor. Maybe years of training would now be really used. The first salvo flew out towards the Ostend shoreline, then another, and the pounding went on. The sky aglow with flashes loomed over the trailing smokescreen.

The smell of cordite and the fracas of engagement drove the artillery on. The shells coming from the shore had not yet found their range. Surreal flashes in the sky, captured second after second by the camera of his own retina, caused him to pause. He surveyed the spectacle: a multicoloured, deafening, and suffocating naval combat. This was the moment, and man's survival seemed to hang on these eternally recurring moments. Moments of heart and reason, moments of masses and individuals, moments that seemed to come from nowhere, but moments that were due to lead somewhere.

A sudden crescendo of fire and explosions came from the north-eastern coastline. The blockship was going into Ostend. It was destined to close up the canal from Bruges and thwart the passage of German raiding ships. William helped load, ram and fire to occupy the German coastal defences and to prevent them turning all they had on the raid.

If war were now his reason and also his heart, then what would happen to him when it was all over? All his youth had been dedicated to readying for war. Would he be able to deal with peace?

After the engagement in the early hours before the dawn broke, William found himself clearing the deck as the Monitor headed back to her berth off Dunkirk.

As he worked, he remembered his father's words to him about the time *he* was sent back from Cannes to England, barely a youth, to live, work and study in the West Country on his grandfather's farm.

'You know, Will, when I came back in '81, I wasn't even a youth, but it was hard because my roots seemed to want to settle down in a different climate and in a different culture. The colours, the noises and scents of the south of France somehow found their way into my blood. I think I'd go back there, if I could, but now your mother and I have seemed to have found a place in life here.'

He paused and recalled what must have been his father's conclusion.

'I get the feeling that man seems to be made to wander and explore, and the only boundaries he really has are those he inflicts on himself and others.'

William contemplated his father's words once again.

Now war had drawn even stronger lines between peoples, and stronger bonds amongst their own. Darkness had descended upon the country and all were duty bound to bear the uniform. The newsreels and films recounting stirring tragedies backed by the marching songs held the country together. The carnage had become Tipperary and kit bags.

Tipperary and kit bags, he thought.

Gunner Bacon handed him a shovel and they cleared the sand off the deck. The sand was spread on decks to absorb the blood and body fluids of men blown up in action. Both men knew it well. They had clocked up another engagement and come through safe from enemy fire.

'It's a dog eat dog existence, this war, isn't it?'?

'I beg your pardon.'

'I mean, those Huns on the end of our shells are the same as us Tommies on the end of their shells.'

'You might say that,' Bacon replied. 'In any case, I suppose, it's all a roll of the dice. Some get lucky. Some don't.'

'You got a family?'

'Not yet, but if we all get out of this alive . . .'

'Oy, you two, this isn't a tearoom. Finish that deck,' came a call.

'Sir!'

As the two men swept the sand up, carried the munitions, cleared the gun turret, William remembered the face of the girl with a shock of chestnut-brown hair and a button-nose who had bumped into him for the first time when he had emerged from his father's public house years ago, and who now seemed likely to play a significant role in his life.

* * *

The next morning William Halden senior stood in the sunshine on the doorstep of his pub and greeted locals, unaware that his own son had just spent the night pounding the German-held shoreline of Ostend. The news found its way into the newspapers the following day.

La Marne

Chapter 40

1918

Part of the Hampshire Regiment was sitting on a train pulling out of Mondicourt in the Somme. It was past midnight and the train creaked and strained as the steam engine gradually gathered pace in the heavy summer rain. In the paltry light of the carriage, Frank Collis looked at his Private's uniform and thought it was not really as smart as it had looked when he and Gertrude and Harold had been to the photographer's. There Mr. Blair had taken the inevitable, ceremonial, military, family photo. Gertrude had told him he looked lovely and that she was proud of him, and Harold just scampered about until he could be picked up and settled by the photographer. All that was back in January.

Here everybody was wearing the same. Even the officers with their distinctive markings and sleeve-braids merged into the general mass of dimly lit khaki. The train shook again, and Frank turned to the companion riding with him in the carriage, Holly.

'Where are we going, do you reckon?' asked Frank.

'Apparently it's somewhere around the other side of Paris,' Holly replied. 'Now we've cleared them out of the Somme again, it's back to the Marne . . . that's the rumour.'

The two soldiers slumbered through the July night and awoke early as the train came to a halt somewhere on the eastern outskirts of the city of Amiens. People were passing round food, but the water was scarce. The heat cranked up as the sun reached its zenith. Men put blankets on the windows to keep the carriage cooler.

Frank looked out of his window and nudged Holly.

'Nothing but wheat fields and more wheat fields.'

The sun bore down.

'I've never seen such open spaces,' he continued. 'They go on forever.'

Church spires, stations, and train yards came into view and disappeared. Frank checked the time on the large platform clocks. On some platforms men in shirt-sleeves stood expectantly with porter's barrows and gazed as the convoy rolled through. Nobody alighted, so they retired to the shade of the station canopy and the wooden bench and struck up another speculative conversation with the mail boy. The railway staff wore uniforms, too.

When the train finally arrived in Sommesous, the men were ordered out into the waiting army lorries and buses driven by Annamese and Senegalese. They smiled and nodded at the soldiers.

Frank felt disorientated and tired. The journey had taken a day and a half and the different halts on the way came at the wrong times. Nevertheless, the soldiers had waved at passers-by and townsfolk at railway crossings. The worried faces of the population seemed to turn to expressions of relief as they saw the numbers of men travelling to the front. The soldiers also took heart.

Now they bumped along a never-ending straight road lined by plane trees, ashes, elms and oaks.

'The fields go on forever and so do the roads,' he murmured to Holly.

Finally, they reached their destination, Athis.

Frank descended from the lorry, looked up at the remarkable wooded hillsides and the vineyards just below. The sound of military engagement then reached his ears: artillery pounding, a dozen kilometers away, up in the *Montagne de Reims*. The men set up camp and bathed in a nearby river. They had two days to prepare. The roads around the town were dusty, the sun exacerbated the dust, and water was all the men really needed. They had been billeted in a manor farm outside of the town.

As Holly and Frank sat in front of their tent, Private Broad emerged from his and joined them. They didn't know Broad well, but the three men had much in common including looks and a semi-rural, small-town background and outlook on life.

'Sunday. Day of the Lord, rest and prayer,' said Broad.

'You mean, it's back to work tomorrow?' retorted Holly.

'Call it work?' added Frank.

'Call it what you want. It sounds bloody awful up there,' Holly said, pointing to the hillside.

'Well, tomorrow at eight I'd be on my round and delivering,' said Frank.

'Where's that?' asked Broad.

'Maydurham. Got a kid and wife back there. Can't wait to get back.'

'Me too. My folks are in Southampton.'

Retorts of artillery fire broke their concentration. They

looked at a hole in the hedgerow around the small manor farm and watched sparrows flit in and out of a nest.

'When we get up there, we stick together. Alright?' said Holly.

* * *

The following day the regiment left the camp and began their long march towards the front line, passing over the Marne on a newly built engineering bridge, and gradually up the flanks of the hill and into the forest. The forest paths brought shade, greenery, and views of tall grasses, green saplings, spruces and higher broadleaf trees, and multiple patches of blue sky which seemed to beckon to them as they advanced. They were now crossing groups of Italians and French who had left the frontline to regroup and recover. They saluted each other. The smiles were founded on relief for some and the hope that their camaraderie would ensure success for others. Whatever awaited them was the great unknown. Frank felt his backpack and rifle move to regular motion.

Just like clockwork. Except I don't know if we're making time, or if time is making us.

He said the same to Holly, and Holly looked at him askance.

'What ever do you mean?'

'It doesn't matter,' said Frank. 'Bit like when I'm on my rounds. You know, you forget what you're actually doing. Just going through the motions.'

'You better concentrate soon, because the enemy won't let you daydream,' Holly advised.

'Thanks for reminding me.'

They finally reached Germaine. The soldiers looked up at the *mairie* and church that stood quiet and somehow proud, or even indifferent. Hundreds of soldiers from different brigades and artillery pieces advanced on each other. French and Italians streamed out of the forest. It was chaos. The sound of firing was ever nearer. The dusty roads and slopes had taken their toll. The evening began to set in. The men were tired, and tomorrow would be the start of a new ordeal. The rotation of fresh men now meant it had become Frank's turn along with hundreds of others in their sector, and thousands in the whole Marne area. Their only objective: to drive the Germans back out of the *Vallée de l'Ardre* and the Chateau-Thierry salient. Overnight Frank's regiment would move along the forest road, '*rue de Courtagnon*', and attack in the morning.

Meanwhile, standing in the glade at the forest entrance, Frank and Holly watched the chaos as the artillery tried to drive between the constant flow of soldiers and medical convoys returning from Courtagnon with the wounded. Soldiers poured out of the forest only for others to take their place.

Only at midnight did the regiment finally manage to advance along the seven-kilometre stretch. They reached and assembled at the farm in Courtagnon some six hours later. The road was packed with transport, guns, tanks and more troops.

The wheat stood high in the fields running down from the forest to the river hidden by its own trees and bushes as it secreted its own route through the valley past Pourcy and Marfaux. The ears of wheat waved as a breeze came up from the south-east and caught the crops, and the soldiers moved out.

Eight o'clock and may God help us.

They advanced quickly below the barrage from the rear and spread out from the river to the upper reaches of the hill and overlooking wood. Then the German artillery hit, and the wheat field blew up dust, stone, chalk and dirt. Frank made it to the first farm buildings and the men watched as their shells hit the edge of the forest trying to reach the hidden enemy's light artillery and the machine-gun nests. The trees shattered and snapped; plumes of smoke rose. The battalion waited and watched. The men noticed the appalling smell that wafted down the hillside. The horse carcasses from previous engagements still lay in the field.

Frank heard the whistle and saw his fellow soldiers alongside moving out of the cover and joined them. Artillery and machine gun fire shredded the wheat field. They flattened themselves into the wheat in an attempt to catch a furtive view of their enemy's positions. More wheat debris, dirt and stone fell on them. The ridge of the undulating field was the dividing line between being seen or remaining invisible. The enemy waited above them in the vineyards and neighbouring forest edge. The thick crops of wheat were a paltry means of protection and disorientated the men very quickly. Only the tree line and the slope enabled them to gauge their direction. The road below had become invisible and the roofs at Pourcy appeared only to disappear with the uneven terrain.

A German machine gun post on the hill to Frank's right blew up, and he caught sight of a pocket of Senegalese searching the area. Apparently, it had been a single gunner. The men moved on.

Marfaux was down to the battalion's left, but from Cuitron, a couple of buildings higher up, the enemy covered the valley with enfilade fire. It was clear from the screams of the wounded and the numbers killed that until the enemy was removed from there or drawn out of the woods above, there would be no end to the battle. German artillery and machine gun fire from Marfaux raked the field, again.

'Halt! Men, halt!' shouted Lieutenant Scott. Scott looked around and tried to estimate range. A dip in the field sited above the road down to their left seemed appropriate. The men descended to escape from the enemy fire.

'Dig in. Marfaux's full of 'em and we have to consolidate here. With luck, if we join the attack on Marfaux from the west, it will eventually drive the blighters out.'

Frank helped Broad and the Labour corps dig feverishly into the dry soil and as night fell the dead and wounded were carried behind the lines to Pourcy. The night was still warm. The smell of the wheat field and the men's sweat hung over the makeshift defence. The stench of the dead horses churned the men's stomachs.

Early next day Frank looked at Broad and asked him what the hell they were doing there and Broad just looked blank.

'You know what?' said Broad. 'Out here it's just two environments, nature versus man and man versus man, and I know which side I'd be on if I could choose.'

'Yep, I reckon I'd rather be a stinging nettle in the forest right now,' Frank retorted. 'You've been to hell and back in the Somme. I'm a latecomer. Honestly, I don't know how you do it?'

'Being a nettle doesn't stop you from getting blown to bits.'

The sound of machinery reached their ears and gradually French tanks hauled themselves into view on the road below and passed them by. A sudden flurry of soldiers on bicycles followed.

'ANZAC's', said Broad. 'They were in the forest the other day. Heard them speaking.'

'Don't ride my postbike that fast!'

'Dodging bullets, you have to, mate.'

Then orders were given to move up a number of men to skirt the woods to drive out the Germans. The others would split from the group with a view to taking Cuitron, which stood in the centre of the action. The men climbed out of their holes and took to the wheat fields again. Sunny skies projected beams of light and pure vision down on to the theatre of action. Broad and Frank moved forward gradually keeping an eye on the village ahead. Broad was ordered up the hill in the attack on Cuitron's two houses and a copse. Frank was ordered up the hill towards the woods. The two men gave the thumbs-up and separated.

Frank brushed through the wheat. He knelt, then watched and followed the battalion as it wheeled up the slope and skirted the safe edges of the woods in small groups next to the Senegalese. Then an indentation formed a 'V', almost a right angle, in the line of the forest. The enemy was virtually opposite in the shattered trees and forest debris. Their orders were to wait to see the enemy clearly before opening fire. The German division was already on its last legs and terribly stretched, so it had to make every bullet count. Here it had the topographical advantage, but the force of numbers was stacked against them.

The ground was dry and dusty. The men sent up clouds of grey as they attempted to surprise the Germans. The enemy still couldn't be seen despite the artillery barrage occupying them. The allied infantrymen advanced. Shells fired from the rear hit the German positions. The bushes and trees shattered, creaked and fell. Branches caught falling branches and foliage crashed around the edge of the wood. Several enemy machine gun nests were revealed, and the battalion moved towards them. Frank could see a group of German gunners on the edge of the wood and remembered the adage, *if you can see them, they can see you*. He ducked down and lay in the wheat. The man in front fell, caught by bullets to his legs.

'Let's go men, charge!' the lieutenant shouted.

Frank's men kept just outside the forest's edge. He caught sight of a Senegalese. He was waving his coupe-coupe and split a machine-gunner's head. For a split-second the sight captured Frank's attention.

Blue sky. A hot spark somewhere landed on his forehead like splattering boiling water, another burn caught his cheek and he tried to call out as the ground gave beneath his feet. His legs had collapsed for no reason. He held on to the stones, dirt and chalk. A man ran by. Then another, then another. Shouts and more shouts. The blue sky engulfed him, the wheat field held him, and the sounds of firing and explosions grew louder, but his body was no longer answering. He felt the wheat stalks through his uniform, his face against the rough ground, the smell of soil and chalk, and wondered why he couldn't get up.

* * *

The door opened and he held out a postcard to Gertrude. She was young and pretty and held a little boy. It seemed her hair was so wiry and curled that there was nothing she could do with it. She gave him a smile and retreated. He tried in vain to speak to her. The little boy waved. He returned to his bike and pedalled towards the town.

Maydurham

Chapter 41

By mid-August Gertrude had still not received any news from Frank. Rose had heard of her worries and had come to take Harold and Gertrude for a walk. She pulled the doorbell to her sister's terraced house.

When Gertrude appeared, it was clear that anxiety had taken its terrible toll. Harold stood by her holding her hand and pleased to take a kiss from Rose. They stood in the passageway leading to the kitchen. Rose listened to her worries; no news may be a sign of fighting or movements, but no news for such a long time she could not understand, especially since they had been able to exchange fairly regularly over the previous months. Now the correspondence seemed to have come to a halt.

'Surely if something has happened to him, they would let me know?' she said to Rose as she beckoned her to look at the last card from the Forces mail.

'Of course, but maybe they're on the move now, you know.'

'No, Rose, the cards pass, the messages have stopped.'

Harold looked at his mother and examined the anxiety and tension that ran across her furrowed brow and drained her looks.

'Let's go out, Gertie.'

The two women packed a little basket and took an old bed cover. They walked over the railway bridge, up the hill and crossed the fields holding Harold by the hand or carrying him. They found themselves at the top of the lanes at the village church.

'Shall we try the Shoulder of Mutton?'

'If you want. Harold, shall we go up the hill?'

The summer day was warm and encouraging. Harold knew they would put the old cover down and eat his mother's cakes when they reached the top.

The view from the top took in the manor house, the church and the town spire in the distance. The sun was still high, and the three figures found others coming down; it was a local pilgrimage. Nature was waiting for nobody, but the groups came and surveyed the wondrous scene trying to find the features in the landscape and distant buildings. The three figures sat down and handed around some cakes and a bottle that Gertrude had brought in her basket. As they lay back in the sun, Harold grew restless and climbed the last few yards to the edge of the copse above them and slipped under the fence into the trees. Gertrude called him back down. Rose went up to check and found him with his hands in the dirt.

'What are you doing, Harold?'

He crawled back through the fence clutching a small disc, which appeared worse for wear and from which a delicate rusty chain dangled. Rose took it from him, and Harold raised his hands and pleaded to keep it.

They came back down the hill and showed it to Gertrude.

'Looks dirty to me,' said Gertrude. 'Must have been

dropped a long time ago. It looks like a dog tag. No name though.'

Harold held out his hand.

'Please, Mummy. Can I have it?'

'We'll take it home and clean it. Well done, you've walked all the way up the hill. Go carefully on the way down.'

'I'm tired of waiting,' said Gertrude as she folded the blanket. 'I'm sure something's happened to him.'

They rose and started their journey back down to the town.

* * *

Some ten days later the telegram came. He had been killed in action. More than a month ago.

Gertrude was inconsolable. She wept for hours on end and wished that she could just see Frank one more time; his usual fair-haired face, his long features and unassuming gentleness. Who would hold her and Harold in his arms now? A blanket of emptiness seemed the only response. Olive and Gertrude, both only few years into their marriages, had already lost everything.

After the terrible, empty and gruelling wait for news, she now wanted to know everything and wrote to the War Office, including the number they requested. Why hadn't he written for so long? Had he died after a long period in the field hospital? Why had it taken them more than a month to let her know?

Louisa came to stay and help with Harold. Friends and the new neighbours spent time with her. She wrote to the

Enquiry Department for the Wounded and Missing but none could help her. The department could only draw blanks.

* * *

Harold knew something was terribly wrong and Daddy was in the middle of it. Everybody held him tight. Rose and Olive took him out. Grandmother brought him toys.

Shortly after the Battle of the Ardre the war gradually took a new turn. The enemy retreated mile after mile and it was now just a question of time before it was all over. In the end Gertrude kept it all to herself. More than a hundred men from the town had been lost, and many including Olive had experienced the horrors of the loss of a loved one at sea. The family was never really demonstrative; it was made of modest people who toiled, full of cares and occasionally a little hope. They had understood the thin boundary that divided them all from the darkness.

Gertrude was allocated a war widow's pension and tried to get on with her life. Harold meant more than anything to her.

* * *

In a prison camp near Soltau unbeknown to Freddie and Gertrude, some six hundred miles away Drummer 'Sammy' Soloman gave up the ghost. Tuberculosis had gone on the rampage through the prison camp one month and a half before the end of the war. Charlie's family had lost two sons.

PART 5

Pack up your troubles

Maydurham

Chapter 42

When the war was over and a large number of troops had returned, thousands of widows and families were still trying to find out what had happened to their loved ones. Gertrude had written several times and received letters from the War Office explaining that, for the moment at least, they could not help. In January, however, a letter came from the War Office quoting a certain Private Broad.

'I knew Private Frank Collis in 'A' Company. He was formerly a postman in Maydurham. On 22nd July I saw him lying in the open badly wounded by bullets to the head. It seemed a hopeless case. I heard from Private Holly that he later died from his wounds.'

Frank's body would not be repatriated. He would lie in a British Cemetery, in the same way as hundreds of thousands, in a 'foreign field'. Gertrude had grown to expect something like this; numerous rumours and tales had circulated with similar stories of letters from servicemen.

She put the letter in her pocket and dressed Harold who had recently turned three and walked him to the photographic shop. The weather was bitterly cold, and she was grateful for the warmth of the new photographer's interior. Mr. Blair had died several months ago.

'I am sorry to hear your news,' said the shopkeeper.

'Please accept my condolences. I know they won't bring him back, though.'

'Thank you, I know. I was wondering if you could make some prints for me, please?'

'Of course, may I see?'

'How many?'

'I think three will do. The same size as this.'

Gertrude handed over a negative and a photo and the new photographer told her to come back the next morning.

The following afternoon Louisa opened her door and Gertrude, Mabel and Harold stood there.

'I've just been to the photographic shop to pick this up. And I received this yesterday,' said Gertrude showing her the photo and the letter from the War Office.

Louisa read the letter and sighed. Mabel took Harold to the back room and cut up an apple for him. Gertrude stood in front of Louisa's newly mirrored mantelpiece and placed a newly framed picture of herself, Frank, and Harold.

'How are you taking it, sweetheart?' asked Louisa.

'In some way I have always expected news like this but it's still too vivid when you actually get it.'

She paused and changed the subject: 'So, you finally got a mirror put up and there's still room for the photos?'

Gertrude stepped back and returned to the mantelpiece, moved the different frames about and finally decided to place hers next to that of Tom and Olive.

'Harold! Come and do the photos with grandma.'

Louisa picked him up and the boy ran through the names without omitting a single one.

'You know the last time you told me about getting a mirror . . .'

'Yes, I remember,' said Louisa. 'It was ten years ago.'

'That's a long time.'

'Hard to forget. Now I can look at myself,' said Louisa, checking her hair.

'I try to,' said Gertrude. 'Who's that little boy in the mirror?' she said to her son.

'Hawuld,' said the boy.

Louisa put him down and Gertrude, Mabel and Harold made their way towards the Square. Ada was cleaning the windows inside the pub and waved. She saw Harold and came outside and pressed tuppence into his hand.

'There you are, sweet. I missed him for Christmas, Gertie.'

'Never mind, thank you.'

Harold looked up at Ada. She examined him.

'Got his father's looks.'

'How's Lyndsey?'

'Busy, he never stops. Still thinks we'll make it to France one day. And William Henry's in Murmansk somewhere. They're still fighting the Bolsheviks.'

Mabel looked across the Square at the church.

'Well, must be going, it's getting cold. Bye, Ada.'

They took their leave and Harold turned and waved.

Battersea

Chapter 43

Dorothy, Miss Maud's sister-in-law, was young and had enthusiastically helped with funds for the foster children in Mrs. Watkins' care. The age difference between the two women was significant and Dorothy looked up to her writer sister-in-law respectfully. Constance Maud was the committed social conscience as much as her brother Philip was the committed Edwardian African explorer. Dorothy as his spouse was duty bound to follow. She came from the vicar of Claydon's family and had received an education at *Northlands*, a school of general education for young ladies run by Sophie Weisse, with a strong emphasis on the arts.

Married to Constance's brother at twenty-two, tragedy struck when she was barely thirty-six, which left a hole in the finances that were available to Miss Maud for the upkeep of Freddie, Betty and 'Daisy'.

She had received the message from her brother informing her of the terrible news and, as the reality sank in, it was clear that Miss Maud would need to find further help. The family was shaken, and few could come to terms with the unexpected and fearful end to the life of Dorothy Maud.

Then Constance Maud's awful reality collided with another as she paid a visit to Mrs. Watkins.

They sat in her front room one July afternoon and Mrs. Watkins explained her predicament.

'I really don't know how to put this, but we have had Fred now for the best part of six years and more and it's not that he's rude or troublesome or misses school . . . anyway he wouldn't . . . and I know he's got a good heart and is clever . . . but he's been taking food . . . stealing food . . .'

'What do you mean, stealing food?'

'Well, the other day . . . I caught him taking food from the pantry and it's not the first time. I realise he must be hungry . . . and, look, I am sorry to have to say this, but we only just about manage to get by and I can't take care of everybody properly, if Freddie steals. The other day I was preparing breakfast and saw that nearly half of a loaf had gone overnight.'

Miss Maud looked out of the window and wondered about Freddie's stealing and its context.

'Are you saying you will not be able to manage Freddie?'

'I don't know. Maybe, if there had been a man in the family, he would have found his feet a little better, you understand, maybe there would have been a different means of persuasion?'

She turned her gaze to the mantelpiece and stood up to fetch the photo. Both women knew the picture well.

'It's him there in his sailor's uniform. Can you imagine? He can only have been four years old. Rose was so proud when she sat there with the three of them. She's been called 'Auntie Rose' all this time and she's still so young, just fifteen. They're as much her children as mine.'

Miss Maud felt the wave of emotion in Hannah

Watkins' voice and tried to keep the substance of their conversation going.

'Yes, it's hard to see Freddie differently today since he has always had good points, poor little fellow and very good brains. I was wondering . . . do you think he might return to the Mission and spend some time under the supervision of a master there? To get him back on the rails, so to speak, you know.'

She paused.

'Actually, Mrs. Watkins . . . I came here to tell you, too, that I am now faced with a problem for the upkeep of the three of them. We have had a terrible ordeal in our family, and I wanted you to know that I will do all I can to keep going, but . . .'

Mrs. Watkins misunderstood the full weight of Miss Maud's message. Miss Maud had not mentioned money.

'I do love him, and I would prefer to look after him, too.'

'I'm sure you do and it's best for him, too. But . . . unless . . .'

Miss Maud's suddenly eyes lit up. Maybe she would not have to mention money.

'You know, Mrs. Watkins, I wonder if I couldn't find help from somebody I know.'

'You mean, somebody who might help you with your ordeal . . .?'

'Maybe, yes. Now, look, if I can continue to help, I will. I promise.'

Miss Maud left the house and crossed the bridge towards her current dwelling further north towards Brompton. The walk was certainly longer but enabled her to run ideas through her mind for the children. The two women had talked at crossed purposes and nothing had been made clear.

Her friend Miss Milner had been staying in the family apartments in Brompton where she was now heading. She was a woman of means and a good friend. For the time being Miss Maud could just about cope, but help would be needed no doubt in the coming year.

The gentle July breeze warmed the banks of the Thames and the plane trees hanging over the water's edge. The perspectives of Battersea Park and its lake were hidden by the trees, too, but the shouts of the carefree rowers and boating community on the lake gave the afternoon a sense of holiday.

'We have to do all we can for these children,' she said to herself. 'They have had very little to shout about in their lives so far, so the rest has to work out somehow.'

* * *

Several months later Mrs. Willis and Miss Hurd gained knowledge of Miss Maud's difficulties and decided to see if they could pursue the matter in another direction. This time they touched on the subject of having Freddie adopted.

The Mission was able to provide a large number of children to childless couples, but Freddie's case was a little different. Miss Hurd had started the ball rolling, but Mrs. Willis still failed to see the advantage.

The two women sat in their office having just ushered a lost young pregnant girl out of the door of their darkened room and into the arms of one of the nurses from the Lodge.

'Now Miss Hurd, what were we saying about young Freddie Foster?'

'You mean, adopting Freddie?' came the reply.

'Adoption, Miss Hurd? It's a bit drastic don't you think?' Mrs. Willis said with an earnestness that cut Miss Hurd a little short.

She continued:

'The boy is nearly eleven and bound for secondary education and we would be asking a couple to take him at this age. I am fairly sure that we must pursue with Mrs. Watkins and if necessary, try to find another benefactor. You know Miss Hurd, I must say that you do have some bold ideas, if, that is, you don't mind my saying.'

'Not at all,' Miss Hurd offered meekly.

Miss Hurd recoiled and realized that she had once again slightly overstepped the limits of Mrs. Willis's propriety when it came to children's education and nurturing. She had helped numerous couples before with adoption, but all with infants or babies. Eleven-year-old children hadn't yet come into her sphere.'

'I am sorry, Mrs. Willis, but I was thinking about avoiding the young lad becoming a child migrant, especially if we are unable to cover his upkeep and Mrs. Watkins and Miss Maud are having problems with him.'

'And who were you thinking of for migration? Barnardo's? '

'I really hadn't considered that aspect . . . as I said . . .'

'Well, please don't consider it. At least not for the moment.'

'Shall I write to Miss Maud to see if she has suggestions for further benefactors?'

'That, Miss Hurd, would be a little more appropriate, I feel.'

Miss Hurd was a great deal younger than Mrs. Ransome Willis and bowed to the wiser head.

'Home Children are a last resort, Miss Hurd, a last resort.'

Miss Hurd still couldn't really get over the name 'Home Children'. After all, 'Home children' and migration seemed rather like an oxymoron. She would send a message to Miss Maud the next day.

'Another thing, Miss Hurd,' continued Mrs. Willis. 'If we go as far as to have young Freddie sent to Australia, then it will be under the condition that both of his parents are dead, or at least that's what he must be told. And we both know full well that that may certainly not be the case. Miss Kimble is most certainly still alive.'

Miss Hurd tried to picture herself telling the boy that he was going to Australia, because his parents were dead, and that Mrs. Watkins was no longer able to keep him. She shrank from the thought and considered writing an even fuller letter to Miss Maud.

Claydon

Chapter 44

Miss Maud's idea that one of her friends may help in funding her three fostered children was overtaken by her unexpected illness. Operation succeeded operation and finally the first sunshine of spring that year breathed new life into her mental and physical faculties and gave her the will to move forward with her life and that of others. Freddie was now coming twelve years old and had been back in the Mission under the care of a master for the best part of a year.

The banks of the Thames provided colour and perspective to her slowed and yet determined figure as she crossed the bridge in London SW 3. Today she was bound for the railway station at Clapham on her way to the Mission's offices in Claydon where she would meet Miss Hurd and Mrs. Willis at Hirst House. Freddie would be there.

In their office, the two women awaited Miss Maud. Mrs. Willis was worried.

'The figures aren't all that good, either, I'm afraid to say, Miss Hurd. We are now twenty-five thousand in debt and Mr. Begly just keeps on saying, 'consolidate, consolidate!' But you know when you are in this kind of work you have to go on and on. There's no stopping . . . there can't be, dare I say, until sin stops. You know as well as I do, for every despairing woman in our maternities and happy child in our nurseries there are three or four future mothers knocking at our doors. All we can do is trust in the Almighty and go on.'

Miss Hurd knew full well that there would be no alternative other than to keep racking up debt until a wealthy benefactor or a chance inheritance provided help and despite her position, she was also aware that the Haven was operating outside the law.

Miss Maud alighted at South Claydon and walked up the steps, over the footbridge and directly into Hirst House. She was aggrieved. The letter from Miss Hurd rankled, especially after all the years of support she had provided.

'I have been wondering whether you would consider having little Freddie adopted. He is a very nice little boy, and on thinking things over it seems to me a really suitable case for adoption . . .'

Yours faithfully,

Children's Secretary.

As she rang the bell, she thought that the Children's Secretary was wielding more power over the lives of the little ones than she should be endowed with. Why had Mrs. Willis not been the respondent? And why had Freddie become 'it' and 'a case'?

The bell interrupted the fraught conversation carried on by the two ladies.

'I am certain that Miss Maud is opposed to the idea of adoption,' said Miss Hurd.

'I am not surprised. You should have couched that letter in better terms, Miss Hurd.'

Miss Maud was ushered in and stood between the two women from the Mission. The two elders were of the same age and Miss Hurd felt herself a little out of place between two seniors and the wiser perspectives of their generation.

'Welcome, Miss Maud, please take a seat. Miss Hurd, will you ask June to make some tea for us, please. You will have a cup of tea, Miss Maud, won't you?'

'Thank you, I will. It is a nice place you have here,' said Miss Maud.

'Thank you for saying so. We have a number of homes now and we hope they will all meet the standards for the mothers and children. Freddie's here, as you already know.'

'I must say that you do a remarkable job, Mrs. Willis, and I am most grateful to you for bringing Freddie back into the Mission, but I must confess that my heart has driven me here first of all to query what Miss Hurd has written to me. Maybe you saw the letter . . . You see, she asks about a possible adoption when I am already his guardian and I have had him in my charge for seven years now, and, as you know, last year when Mrs. Watkins found him too disobedient the Mission took him over and today I pay ten shillings a week for him to you! And as far as I can establish, this seems to be working out if I am not mistaken.'

Mrs. Willis looked on and gave Miss Maud her enigmatic Mona Lisa-like smile. A sign that led Miss Maud to continue.

'Well, what exactly do you suggest for Freddie? Does he need to be adopted? And who by?'

She paused, but Mrs. Willis was not forthcoming.

'As you know, I wanted him, Betty, and Rose to have a happy home life with Mrs. Watkins, and at sixteen to help ensure that he would find an employment that suited him best. He'll be twelve next month and we must not falter.'

'Yes, Miss Maud, I fully understand, and you are certainly right, we must not falter. And The Mission will not. We have a considerable responsibility to many children and child mothers in the maternity homes and nurseries, and now with the education of the infants and older children. And, as you so rightly said, Freddie is now back amongst us and is our responsibility. You must understand, too, that the Mission is now his prime source of welfare and education.'

Miss Maud leant forward about to express herself when June came through and placed a tray between the two ladies.

'I appreciate that, as I said, but I do not see how adoption may be a solution to his upsetting spell with Mrs. Watkins. What I didn't really appreciate was that, according to Miss Hurd, Freddie has now become, a 'case', an 'it' rather than a 'he'.'

She produced Miss Hurd's letter. Mrs. Willis re-read it.

'I *am* sorry that you should take it like that. I am sure that Miss Hurd probably has much to do and sometimes places expediency ahead of careful phrasing.'

'I am sure that must be the case, but it is hurtful to read rather loose remarks like that, nevertheless.'

Mrs. Willis considered her colleague's words and realized that Miss Maud's anxiety could be defused, if she saw her ward.

'Shall I take you to see Freddie?'

The two women made their way around the house to a wooden out-building which had once been a big storage shed and now, refurbished, acted as a common-room for the youngsters.

'Freddie,' called Mrs. Willis. 'There's someone here to see you.'

Miss Maud dreaded the use of that phrase.

Freddie looked around. His dark short curly hair, broad forehead and dark eyes looked in the direction of the two ladies. He left the small group turning over pages in a stamp album and stood before them. Miss Maud asked if she could speak to Freddie in private. A moment alone with Freddie would help her to feel her way through the current situation. The wooden panelling of the room and the confrontation of the three persons produced the effect of time standing still and nothing happening, so she held her hand out and walked Freddie to the courtyard.

'Do you remember me?' asked Miss Maud.

Freddie had recollections of her visits to 'Mum's' and 'Aunty Rose's'.

'Yes, a little bit.'

'How do you like it here?'

'It's all right.'

'Would you rather be back in Battersea with Mrs. Watkins?'

Freddie nodded his broad forehead.

'*Only a boy*,' thought Miss Maud. '*Only a boy bobbing about like a cork on changing currents and tides trying to keep himself on an even keel.*'

She realized that the whole affair was more like a human laboratory experiment and that whatever was said to such a young and sensitive being was likely to be just another blow to his system.

Mrs. Watkins' family had been his only true refuge and set of bearings in the last seven years, and it seemed unlikely that he could go back. Adoption would be the last straw.

'Do you have some good friends here?' she asked. 'Do you miss Betty and Rose?'

He looked across the courtyard and she followed his gaze towards the other boys at the table and the stamps.

'*How could he conceive of tomorrow when the present is his only possession and, for the better part, an unreliable friend?*'

'Freddie, I will come back to see you, but remember to make friends here for the time being and be a good lad, and I am sure things will work out.'

The boy turned to her and smiled. The boy thought he might be going back to 'Mum'. Once again his mind wandered through the promises that adults had made to him all his life.

'Well, I must be going. Take care. I will be back.'

Freddie returned to the other boys and watched as the lady crossed the courtyard holding a handkerchief.

A little later, June carried the cold tea back to the kitchen.

Chapter 45

Miss Hurd paused over the thick letter and its contents lying on her heavy wooden desk. Mrs. Willis had handed it to her. It concerned the possible transportation of *Home Children* to Australia where farmers and people working the land were said to be in need of labour. Young British *Barnardo* boys were welcomed into families and brought up as one of their own. The boys had to be younger than thirteen and a half. The patrons were their Royal Highnesses, the King and Queen.

'Well, you may say that royal patronage is a fine blessing for the idea and perhaps we should also consider that it may be an opportunity for several of our young boys,' she said to Mrs. Willis, who peered over her spectacles in return and contemplated the new idea.

'Certainly, the release of a number of boys will take the strain off the costs for their welfare and education here,' suggested Mrs. Willis

'Furthermore, Mrs. Willis, for that age group adoption is very problematic for boys. Adoption of young girls has always been so much easier.'

'I would assume that you already have somebody in mind?'

'Well, I think we both may have several in mind.'

'Perhaps we might select those we feel can cope and speak to them as a group?' suggested Mrs. Willis.

'Do you think *Barnardo* will take some of *our* boys?'

'I would sincerely hope so, after all, it will help us to develop a link with them, and I do fear for our adoption scheme once the lawmakers get in. It is a Christian endeavor and we know it has no legal basis. The blue forms you give the couples to fill in are worthless in a court of law, and every mother has the right to reclaim her child. We both know that. But if we didn't do what we do, then the world would be even more complex.'

Miss Hurd understood that the Mission was clearly running a fine line.

* * *

Seven boys filtered into the office.

Their looks ranged from curious to blank, from ponderous to keen. Each boy seemed slightly restless that he should be asked to appear before Mrs. Willis. This was rather unusual.

The doyenne left her chair and placed herself squarely before them.

'Boys, we have asked you to come here because we have something to put before you. As you well know, your parents are no longer of this world, God bless them, and your lives here have not been the easiest. You have been lucky insofar as some of you have found a home at The Haven of Hope and some of you have been with foster parents.'

The boys shuffled and some felt that the word, 'lucky', was wrong.

Mrs. Willis pressed on.

'It has recently come to our knowledge that our Australian cousins are keen to welcome groups of young boys such as you to make a new living in their country. This will involve working on the farm and being looked after by Australian farmers or landowners.'

The boy at the front with a broad face, big teeth, glasses and blue eyes was worrying his cap, twisting it in all directions. Clearly, he was anxious.

'Yes, David, what is it? Do you have a question?'

'Are you sending us away?'

'No? David we are not sending you away. We are asking you to think about the idea of going to live and work in Australia. You know the Lord works in many ways and maybe this will be an opportunity for you to fulfill your life as a young man? Would you like to say something, boys?'

They looked at each other, unsure. All their lives they had been moved around or abandoned by adults and now they were being asked to give their thoughts about going across the globe to Australia.

'I don't know, Mrs. Willis, I don't know,' replied David.

Clearly the seven boys had differing views. Mrs. Willis had to engineer a consensus amongst them, so she offered a second hearing on the subject with a man she knew from *Barnardo*, to which the boys agreed.

Having given them several reassurances about their futures, the two women ushered the boys out of the office and pored over a newspaper cutting that was included in the letter.

FIRST BARNARDO BOYS FOR AUSTRALIA.
CONGRATULATIONS FROM THE
KING AND QUEEN

This week forty-seven Barnardo boys departed for Sydney, Australia, and on leaving Tilbury the party sent a loyal telegram to the King and Queen, their patrons.

Their Majesties replied:

> *'The King and Queen are interested to hear of the first party of young boys who are leaving the Mother Country for Australia from the Barnardo Homes. They wish them all good luck with their new home in Australia, of which Dominion Their Majesties, from their own personal experience, preserve the happiest memories.'*

Tilbury

Chapter 46

The Mission bought the boys overcoats and warm wear. The February weather would be tough on the ship until they reached the Mediterranean and the Suez Canal. They all bore the same kind of large square suitcases and cloth caps. The group of Barnardo boys bore a resemblance to a school outing and seemed to behave accordingly. Many of the boys knew each other. Their uniforms were simple: grey jackets, shirts and ties with V-neck pullovers, short trousers and long grey socks. The large group was excited at the idea of a long boat trip.

Miss Maud had insisted that Freddie might spend his last Christmas with Mrs. Watkins' family, but the Mission refused, using the excuse of the risk of his bringing back any illness into the Home and jeopardizing the boys' departure. In the end Freddie had spent his last week with Mrs. Watkins, his five aunts, Betty and Daisy, and they spoiled him, took him to the photographers and gave him a bundle of items to take with him.

On February 20th, 1923, Miss Amelia Willis was also on her way to the dock. She was deputizing for her aging mother. Unaware that the sailing may be brought forward because of the tide and thinking she had plenty of time, she was now at a loss when the official told her that the ship would be manoeuvring soon. She hurried to check the berth and reached the ship just in time.

Adults mixed with the large numbers of children; some would be accompanying them for the organizations they represented, and which now would be setting up offices in Australia whilst others came on board to say, 'goodbye'.

There were cameramen from the press and some children were asked to form a group on the gangway, smile or cheer and wave. The weather was bitterly cold, and the damp permeated the ship's decks.

Amelia Willis mounted the gangway, moved anxiously along the ship's deck and looked for Freddie.

He stood with others, waving at the cameramen below on the quayside.

She carried a message from Miss Maud and pressed it into his hand.

'You will write to her, won't you Freddie? Goodbye, boys. God speed.'

Freddie pushed the letter into his overcoat pocket and continued to wave with the others as they had been asked. He watched as she descended the gangway and looked back at the Mission's boys.

Only when he saw the hawsers loosen and fall into the water did he realize that the adults around him had changed the course of his life once again.

In the afternoon gloom, as the others around him chattered or ran along the deck he looked across at the other London shore of Gravesend and tried to reason why he had never had a mother and father.

* * *

Several days later Miss Maud received another letter from Miss Hurd.

Dear Miss Maud,

Many thanks for your postcard received this morning.

After all, I was unable to go and see the boys off on the 20th. Miss Willis went and I asked her specially to see Freddie and give him your message. This she did.

Freddie said he had had your letter and promised Miss Willis he would write to you.

I am sure you will be glad to know they went off in very good spirits. They sailed from Tilbury about four o'clock in the afternoon and all seemed very excited with the thought of going to Australia.

I am so sorry he did not answer your letter it seems so ungrateful after all you have done for him.

Yours sincerely,

Children's Secretary.

Epilogue

The view overlooking the fields, church steeples, and roofs of the terraced houses grows blurred. The evening has begun to set in and it is time to walk back up the country lane to the main road.

Down in the town, people won't know of this story, nor of these remarkable people who were loath to tell it.

Time worked its way through the hearts of many, but the ink-stain left by the terrible events that this generation suffered never really went away. Notwithstanding, they kept it for themselves.

Children were born and grandchildren arrived, and their story was gradually diluted or became submerged; the younger members of the family had their own lives to lead.

Gertrude and her son, Harold, became inseparable. They spent their happiest moments on Southsea front or Hayling Island with Rose, Mabel, Louisa and the other young ones. Rose lived on with Lupus disease and a disability pension to a very old age. Mabel found her sailor, William Henry Halden, as she had planned. They brought two children into the world: Lindsey and Betty. When William Lyndsey died, Mabel carried on the pub with her mother-in-law, Ada. Freddie spent his first three years in Australia strafing rabbits in the outback and settled with farm people. He wrote to say he wanted to come home but to no avail. Later he married, raised his own family and flew in the Australian

Air Force (RAAF) in World War II. (His two daughters, Beverley and Cheryl along with their husbands, travelled to England in 1994 in the hope of finding out about the roots of their family and discovered a large part of Freddie's story thanks to the descendants of Hannah Watkins).

Olive and Louisa stayed in the background and watched over, as ever.

Fred's 'polymath' activities grew daily to the point where he would one day keep lions and other wild animals in his own backyard. He also continued his brass band and raised three boys. Bill raised four boys and prolonged the Harding side of the family. Part of that family found its way to Australia, too.

Mrs. Willis, Miss Amelia Willis, and Miss Hurd rode out their financial difficulties thanks to a generous benefactor. The Adoption Laws were passed, and after presiding over more than two thousand adoptions, The Haven of Hope's unauthorized handling of adoption was reined in. Miss Amelia Willis certainly reflected on the moments of the boys' departure, having fully realized that the condition *sine qua non* for transportation was the fictional death of the boys' birthmothers, to whom she had been close in the Bible Study classes and whom she knew to be probably alive and well. Her presence with those children at Tilbury and prior to that had formed nothing more than a flimsy wall of deceit between the *lost* 'birth-mother' and the child.

Miss Maud fretted over Freddie and what the span of her life had held, and as its span grew ever shorter it finally folded away just before the Great Crash, while she was still wondering if he would ever send her a letter from Australia.

War memorials were put up all around Europe and people flocked to remember the dead on Armistice Day.

But this is just a list, and sometimes it is difficult to bear all this in mind and wonder how *we* ever got here, and how *they* survived the dreadful ordeals. No doubt, we would forget, were it not for reminders, one of which is to be found on the stone at the top of this hill where the seasons bear down and wear its surface, and from where the wanderer looks out across the downs, farmlands and occasional steeple to the town and row of houses where so much happened, and is thereby reminded that he or she is duty-bound to tell the story.

Then, somehow, we will know.

> *"And I rose up, and knew that I was tired, and continued my journey."*
>
> —Edward Thomas.

Acknowledgements

My thanks go to the following, whose precious help, advice and consideration have been vital to this book.

Jane and Derek Philpot, Barry Sayer, Christine, Bénédicte, Damien and Jonathan Sayer, Beverley and Barry Leaney, Cheryl Brooks, Jill Gallacher and her family, Frank, Anne, David and Peter Sayer, Jo, Stuart and Jonathan Hayden, John Kimber, Diane Chaplin, Peter, Wendy and Sigrid Hardy, Zoe Sloman, John Watkin.

Pierre Bonnand – Montagne de Reims bikes; Callum Brazier – genealogy correspondent; Marie-Hélène Cainaud – Archives Municipales de Cannes; Deborah Cohen – author; Jean-Pierre Colpin – la Mairie de Sommesous; Tony Field and Chris Bacon – The Wardrobe – The Wiltshire Regiment Museum; Kate and James Fairweather, St Anne's; Geoff Fitton and Brian Furless – Somerset Industrial Archaeological Society; Tom Gamble – Writer, France; Divya Ghelani – Editor, Berlin; Susannah Jarvis and Colin Bulleid – Hampshire Regiment Museum; Michael Kouklakis – Essec, colleague and friend; Jonathan Hayden – Literary Agent & Advice; John Jones – Local Broadclyst Historian; Sam Lindley – Bodleian Libraries; Christian Monnier – Impact Real Estate, Cannes; Karen Noad and Robert Neller – Haslemere Museum; Heather O'Connell – Publishing Consultant; Chris Phillips – Aberystwyth University; Kake Pugh – Croydon Historian; Hazel Pullen – Isle of Wight Family History; Roy Swales –

Fleet Air Arm Museum; Heather Tarling – Christian Family Concern; Jean Vedovati – Local War Historian, La Marne; Sophie Yaniw and Ryan Watts – Petersfield Museum.

The staff of the Archives Diocésaines de Cannes, Le Cimetière du Grand Jas de Cannes, La Mairie d'Athis – La Marne.

Croydon Museum, Devon History Society, Devon Records Library, Hampshire Records Library, Somerset Records Library, Petersfield Arts and Crafts Society.

My *professeurs* from the Université de Nanterre.